★ SADDLES, STARS, & STRIPES ★

BLACKWATER CREEK

From the battlegrounds of the Civil War to the California goldfields, the Saddles, Stars, & Stripes series sweeps you back through American history on an unforgettable journey. Each story's very special heroine comes from a different time and culture, but all share a great love of horses and a unique brand of courage.

KINGFISHER
a Houghton Mifflin Company imprint
222 Berkeley Street
Boston, Massachusetts 02116
www.houghtonmifflinbooks.com

First published in 2005
2 4 6 8 10 9 7 5 3 1

LIBRARY OF CONGRESS CATALOGING–IN–PUBLICATION DATA
has been applied for.

ISBN 0-7534-5885-3
ISBN 978-07534-5885-3   .

Printed in Canada
1TR/0705/TCL/PICA(MA)/50LBCM/C

★ SADDLES, STARS, & STRIPES ★

BLACKWATER CREEK

DEBORAH KENT

KINGFISHER

BOSTON

✴ Chapter One ✴

Gripping handholds among the rocks, Erika scrambled to the crest of the ravine. She paused to catch her breath and looked carefully around her. Her ears strained for a telltale crackle in the underbrush, but she heard only the sigh of the wind. "Virag!" she called. "Come on, Virag! It's milking time!"

Where had that empty-headed cow wandered off to now? This was the third time that she'd broken out of the pasture. A week ago old Hart Latham had caught her grazing calmly at the edge of his hay field. "If I catch that bohunk cow of yours in my fields again, I'll shoot her!" Latham had warned when Erika went to fetch her.

Papa told Erika and her brother, Sandor, to keep Virag off Latham's land and not to set foot there themselves. Virag, however, had her own ideas on the subject. She seemed convinced that the wildflowers in Hart Latham's fields were tastier than anything that the Nagys' pasture could offer her.

But Virag wasn't in the hay field this time. She must have strayed even farther. Erika didn't doubt that Hart Latham would shoot her on sight—if a cougar didn't get her first. Erika shoved those thoughts deep into a back corner of her mind. The Nagys couldn't afford the loss of their only cow, not even a troublemaker like Virag.

Pebbles rolled beneath her feet as Erika made her way along the ridge. Soon the ground sloped down to a grassy hollow, just the sort of place that Virag preferred. Virag would go to great lengths to find flowers to munch on. Her tastes had earned her the name Virag—"flower" in Hungarian. Searching and calling, Erika waded through waist-high grass that rippled around her like water. Hidden grasshoppers rasped out their springtime music. A quail rose up at her feet and hurtled away with a cry of alarm. But there was no sign of the spotted cow.

Sighing, Erika started up the next rise, and when she reached the top, she gasped in dismay.

Before her stood Hart Latham's stable, a low-slung log building with a red-tiled roof. Beyond the stable loomed the ranch house itself. She hadn't realized that her search had brought her so deep into Latham's territory. She wondered who would be more furious —Latham or her father—if he knew that she was here. She should get away before anyone caught her! But Erika couldn't tear herself away from what she saw.

Four horses stood in the corral adjoining the stable. Three of them grazed quietly. The fourth, a little sorrel filly, craned her neck over the top of the fence. Erika couldn't resist. She had to get a closer look.

Ever since her family started renting a piece of Latham's land four months ago, Erika had seen horses come and go from his fields. Horse-trading was one of Latham's businesses, in addition to raising cattle and working gold claims on the Stanislaus river. He and his ranch hands bought horses from other traders or caught them in the mountains and broke them to the saddle. With so many people flooding into the hills to look for gold, horses were always in demand.

Each time she saw one, Erika had longed to feed

Latham's horses and curry them. She had yearned to ride them along California's stony mountain trails. Back in Hungary, Erika's grandmother used to tend all the horses in their village. She liked to take Erika along when she went to treat a horse with colic or a mare in foal. "Watch and learn, my *lanyaunoka*," her grandmother would say. "Someday you'll be taking care of these horses, instead of me."

"Yes, Naganya," Erika would say, feeling proud that her grandmother had so much faith in her. But Erika's contact with horses had ended abruptly when she and her family left Hungary two years ago, back in 1847. Until today she had only looked from a distance, silent and wishful.

Erika approached the corral slowly. The horses looked like mustangs, wiry and sure-footed, the sort that ran wild in the mountains. A pinto and two palominos bunched together in the farthest corner, but the sorrel stayed at the fence. Erika stretched out her hand, and the sorrel filly touched it with her velvety nose. Her golden coat glistened, in lovely contrast to her black mane and tail. A name sprang into Erika's mind, the perfect name for this beautiful filly. "Arany!" she said. *Arany* was the Hungarian word for gold.

The pinto and the palominos twitched their ears and watched cautiously. Then the pinto gave a short whinny, and Arany left Erika to join the other horses. As the filly crossed the paddock, Erika saw that she favored her right foreleg. Something was wrong. Erika had to find out what it was.

Latham's fence was almost as flimsy as the fence to Virag's pasture. The gate sagged on its hinges. Erika unlatched it carefully and entered the corral. "*Szegenyem!*" she murmured in Hungarian. "You poor thing! What's the matter? Let me see."

The filly sidled away for a moment, and then she stood still and let Erika examine her leg. Erika ran her hands over the cannon and pastern to the hoof, as Naganya had taught her back in the old country. The front of the foreleg felt warm and swollen along the cannon bone, and the filly flinched away at Erika's touch.

Shinsore, Erika thought. Maybe someone had ridden her too hard, or perhaps she'd been doing some hard running on her own. The cause didn't matter now. But if Arany's problem went untreated, the filly might become permanently lame. No horse trader would feed and stable a lame horse, especially no trader as cruel as Hart Latham. A limp was the same as a death sentence.

If she could tend to the injury, Erika was confident that Arany would be all right. Some of the plants here in California were almost exactly like the herbs Naganya used for treating horses back home. Erika had seen plenty of waybread—one of the surest remedies for lameness in horses. But would she even be allowed to treat Arany? Would Hart Latham even listen to her?

Not much chance of that, Erika thought ruefully. To Hart Latham she and her family were nothing but "bohunks," foreigners from remote lands in faraway Europe. He was happy to take their rent money, but whenever he spoke to them he tried to make them feel small and unwelcome.

Erika stood beside the filly, resting a hand lightly on her withers. She felt Arany's hide quiver beneath her touch. What should she do? She couldn't leave her without trying to help. Could she run home, prepare a salve, and bring it back here? But the wrappings would have to be changed regularly. She would never be able to sneak back day after day. Maybe she could—

"What do you think you're doing?"

Erika whirled around, and Arany was so startled that she flung up her head and bolted away. A squat, red-faced man in mud-spattered overalls glared from the other side of the fence. "I was just—" Erika stammered. "I—"

"You got no business with them horses," the man growled. "Get out of there!"

On trembling legs Erika stumbled from the paddock, barely remembering to shut the gate behind her. The man watched her through narrowed eyes. "You're the renter's girl, ain't you?" he said.

Erika straightened her shoulders. "My father is Laszlo Nagy," she said. "We rent land from Mr. Latham."

"You better see the boss," he grunted, motioning for her to follow him. Erika had no choice but to obey. He led her around the back of the massive stone house and told her to wait at the kitchen door. He disappeared inside, and Erika waited alone. The wall of the house blocked the afternoon sun, and the bushes in the dooryard looked feeble and thin. A chill seeped through Erika's light muslin bodice. She paced back and forth, crossing her arms to try to keep warm. *Why would Hart Latham want to see me?* she wondered. Maybe he had found Virag again. Perhaps this time he had carried out his threat!

At last a shadow fell across the doorway, and Hart Latham stepped outside. He was not a tall man, but he made Erika think of a bear, fierce and powerful on its sturdy hind legs. Latham's shirt and pants were rumpled, and he frowned at her from above a tangled, dark beard.

"It's about time!" he said, glaring. "I thought I'd have to send Maddox to collect!"

"Collect?" Erika repeated blankly.

"Hand it over!" Latham said. "You better have brought the full amount!"

Erika edged away from him, hiding her empty hands behind her back. "I didn't bring anything," she said. "What amount?"

"No excuses this time!" Latham exploded. "Your father's two months behind on the rent! Where is it?"

Erika's stomach gave a sickening lurch. Why hadn't she guessed that the rent was overdue? Instead of working the land, Papa spent all his time at the gold diggings. She knew that they owed money at the store in town. When she worried about it to Papa, he assured her that he'd pay off their debt as soon as he made a strike. Joe Muldoon at the store understood miners, Papa said. He was willing to give them credit, knowing he'd be paid soon enough.

It was one thing to owe money to smiling, paunchy Joe Muldoon. It was quite another matter to fall behind on rent to Hart Latham.

Erika drew a deep breath. "Papa didn't tell me about any rent, Mr. Latham. But listen, one of your horses has a bad leg. The little gold-colored one. I think I can help—"

"It's my horse," Latham interrupted. "What becomes of her is no business of yours."

"But she'll be lame!" Erika tried once more. "The right plants will help her get better."

Latham gave a short laugh. "You have a lot more to worry about than a horse. Go home and tell your father to bring me the rent by tomorrow morning. If he doesn't pay, you and your family can get off my land!"

The earth seemed to tilt beneath Erika's feet. She thought she was going to faint. "No!" she cried. "We'll pay! Give us a chance!"

Suddenly a voice called from inside, a woman's voice, filled with concern. "Hart! What's going on?"

Latham's tone shifted. It was almost gentle as he replied, "Don't worry, Mags. Everything's all right."

Erika knew in an instant that the slender, fair-haired young woman who slipped out the door had to be Mrs. Latham. Papa had mentioned that Latham had a wife, but she was rarely ever seen. Erika thought that she was very pretty, with dimpled cheeks and soft blue eyes. No wonder Latham kept her out of sight, with so many rough-talking, hard-drinking miners around and so few women at the diggings to keep them company.

"I thought I heard a girl's voice," Mrs. Latham said shyly.

"It's only Nagy's girl," Latham said dismissively. "She has to go now."

"Couldn't she stay and visit a while?" Mrs. Latham asked, a hopeful smile lifting up the corners of her mouth.

"Not now. She has a message to deliver for me," Latham said brusquely, with a hard look at Erika. His wife turned reluctantly and slipped into the house again.

Latham looked back at Erika. "Don't just stand there!" he snapped. "Go tell your father what I said!"

Tears stung Erika's eyes. How could she deliver such bad news to Papa? What would he do? If he didn't have the rent money, where would they go?

She ran across the yard, eager to put distance between herself and Hart Latham.

"Tomorrow morning!" he hurled after her, and his words struck her like sharp-edged stones.

✳ Chapter Two ✳

The sun was beginning its slide down the mountains to the west. Erika quickened her steps, anxious to be home before dark. She took the shortest way that she knew, cutting through ravines and crossing the log bridge over Glutton's Gulch. It was a relief at last to know she was back on Nagy land—or at least it was their land tonight.

Where would they all be tomorrow night, if Papa didn't have the rent money? If Papa and Sandor were alone, they could pitch a tent with the other miners at the diggings. But Papa insisted that the camp was no place for a 14-year-old girl. Now that they were in California, he said, his family had to have a real home.

No smoke curled from the cabin chimney, and Erika saw at once that Sandor and Papa had not returned yet. But she was not entirely alone. As she approached the shed that housed the animals, she heard a deep, familiar moo. There at the door stood Virag. She switched her tail and pawed the ground, impatient to be milked.

"Oh, Virag!" Erika exclaimed, patting her bony flank. "Where have you been?"

Virag followed her into the shed as though nothing unusual had happened. "Thank goodness you're safe," Erika chided her as she settled her into the stall. "How did you get out of the pasture again? I wish you could talk! I'd love to hear what you've been up to."

Erika hurried through the milking and carried the sloshing pail to the cool, moss-roofed spring house behind the shed. Then she went to the cabin to wait.

At some point in the unknown past the Nagys' cabin had served as a shepherd's hut. Built of rough redwood planks, it was a two-room structure with a loft tucked beneath the roof. Erika lit the fire to push back the evening chill and began to prepare their simple supper. There was bread and butter, a bit of salt pork, and cabbage from the garden. If she hadn't spent so much time looking for Virag, she would have made soup. Well, when Papa and Sandor heard the news about the rent, food would be the last thing on their minds!

Erika set three plates and mugs on the table and went to glance out the door. Any minute now they should come up from the diggings, leading the gray mule they called George, short for George Washington. They were late tonight; the sun was almost gone now. Maybe—just maybe—exciting news kept them down at Papa's claim. Perhaps they had made a big strike today—or "seen the elephant," as gold seekers put it. Perhaps all their troubles were over at last!

Don't get carried away, she reminded herself. It was more likely that they had stayed to the last possible minute, hoping against hope that today would be the day. They would trudge home weary and discouraged, impatient with George and irritable with each other. If it was up to Sandor, Erika knew, they would have quit weeks ago. But Papa couldn't conceive of quitting. They'd made the long, perilous journey to California in order to find gold. They weren't going to give up now.

Erika went back inside, swept by a sudden wave of

loneliness. If only her mother had lived to see California! If only she was here this minute! They could have wondered together what was taking Sandor and Papa so long and kept each other laughing as they went about their evening chores.

The Hungarian word for Mama—*Anya*—flooded Erika's mind. Anya would have loved the little shepherd's hut perched on this Californian hillside. It was so different from their cozy thatched cottage back in Szolnok, surrounded by rolling fields of barley and wheat. Anya would have seized every chance to step outdoors and breathe in the clean mountain air, to marvel at the vistas of peaks climbing toward the sky. "America will be filled with adventures!" Anya had told her as they set off in the wagon on the first leg of their long, slow journey. "We'll find things in America we never imagined before!"

If Anya was here, Papa would have farmed the land as he planned to in the beginning. Anya wouldn't have let him go off hunting for gold until the harvest was in. A hundred times Papa had told them that America was the land of the free. In America a family could own land, and no one could take it away from them in the way the Austrians had pushed them off their land in Hungary. In America no kings or emperors battled over the borders. In America they would begin a new and glorious life, where anything was possible.

Papa's claim was a patch of ground at Jonah's Branch, a trickle of a creek flowing into the Stanislaus river. No one officially owned the land there, and anyone was allowed to stake a claim in order to search there for gold. You simply measured a square, 30 paces on each side, and drove a stake into each corner. As long as a miner continued to work his claim, he maintained his rights to that chosen spot.

On his second day at Jonah's Branch Papa had found two gold nuggets the size of marbles, simply by turning over stones in the streambed. With the money from that strike, he rented the shepherd's hut from Hart Latham. By the next week he had found enough gold to buy George, the mule, and Virag, the spotted cow. But Papa's strike was merely beginner's luck, as the miners called it. Since then his efforts had yielded nothing but tiny pebbles and flecks of gold dust, hardly enough to pay for flour and lard from Joe Muldoon. And now they owed Hart Latham two months' rent.

From somewhere out in the darkness came George's

hoofbeats and the sound of voices. Erika listened at the door, expecting Papa and Sandor to take the mule to the shed as usual. Instead they left George on the path and rushed to the cabin, both talking at once.

"Erika! We've got it!" Papa cried. "Today is the day! You won't believe—"

"I never thought it would happen!" Sandor exclaimed. "I wanted to leave early this afternoon but—"

"But I said no, we're going to stick to it," Papa broke in. "Wait till you see what we found!"

Stamping the mud off their boots and laughing with joy, they crowded into the cabin. Their excitement filled the tiny room to overflowing. Papa drew a handkerchief from his pocket and shook it out over the table. A shower of golden pebbles danced across the planks. Erika stared, openmouthed. She stretched out her hand and touched one of the shining stones carefully, warily, as though it might melt away beneath her fingertip.

"It's beautiful!" she breathed. "We'll have everything we need now! Everything will be all right!"

"There's more where this came from," Papa assured her. "We only left because it was getting dark."

"It's under an overhang," Sandor explained. "A clump of roots sticks out over the water. I went in with my knife, started prying around, and there it was—as if it was all tucked away in a chest, waiting for us to pick it up."

Papa gathered up the hoard between his cupped hands. "It feels like a pound," he said. "At sixteen dollars an ounce! And this is just the beginning!"

"We can pay all our debts," Erika said, light-headed. "We can take the rent to Hart Latham tomorrow morning."

No one seemed to be listening. Papa let the golden pebbles stream through his fingers onto the table again. They bounced and rolled and finally lay still, forming a pattern like a lopsided star.

Sandor picked up one of the larger stones and turned it over in his hands. "You can tell it's gold by how smooth it is," he said. "And you can feel it if you run it between your teeth." He slipped the stone between his front teeth and moved it back and forth. Erika saw a strange look cross his face. He took the stone out of his mouth, frowning.

"We can collect three times this much tomorrow," Papa was saying. "Once we have a good stash, we'll take it into the bank. Then we can buy land. A farm of our own! No more renting from that scoundrel Latham."

"What's wrong?" Erika asked Sandor in a low voice.

Sandor didn't answer. He picked up another stone and tested it the same way. "Gritty!" He spat the stone onto the floor. "It isn't gold—it's fool's gold!"

Erika stared at him, aghast. "But you said—" she began. "How—"

"What are you talking about?" Papa demanded. "This isn't fool's gold! I tested it myself, out at the creek."

"You tested the first two pebbles," Sandor pointed out. "Those were gold. But what about the rest?"

"I tested them," Papa repeated, as if he was in a daze. "I pounded them between two rocks. They didn't crack; they flattened."

Sandor stepped outside and returned with two rocks from beside the path. Without a word, he placed a golden stone between them and hammered it with all of his might. The stone shattered into fragments. Sandor took another stone from the table and another. Again and again the stones shattered and cracked. In the end only half a dozen of the smallest pebbles passed the test and proved to be real gold.

Papa watched in silence, his head in his hands. Erika felt as though their dreams had been shattered along with the shining stones. At last Papa quietly scooped up the pieces of fool's gold and tossed them out into the night.

Sandor went out to put George in the shed. Papa pulled off his muddy boots and threw them into a corner. He sat motionless, staring at the fire. Sandor returned, slamming the door so hard that the cabin shook. "I've had it!" he fumed. "We're just wasting our time down there, picking up rocks. It's stupid!"

Papa sprang back to life. "What are you saying? You heard that man from New York! Last week he found a nugget this big!" Papa made a wide cup with his hands, as though he was holding a pumpkin.

"You know who's making the real money out of all this?" Sandor lashed out. "It's that fellow who sells the shovels and the pans. He's getting richer by the minute! That's the business we should be in."

"We didn't come all this way to sell shovels!" Papa declared. "I thought I raised you to have more sense!"

Erika sighed. She'd heard the whole debate before. When he was in good spirits, Sandor's eyes sparkled, and he had a winning smile. Lately, though, he'd grown to resent spending day after day at the diggings, and his face was clouded with worry. Now he held up his hands. They were covered with scratches and blisters, and his knuckles were scraped raw. "I'm sick of gold mining," he said fiercely. "I'd be happier selling shovels or axes or feather beds—not wasting time on foolish dreams!"

"Let's sit down and eat," Erika broke in. "What's the use of fighting?"

They began supper in troubled silence. Disappointment hung over them like a dense fog. Erika searched for a way to lighten the mood. "Virag broke out again," she said, forcing a laugh. "I looked all over for her, and when I came home, she was waiting by the shed."

"Where did you look?" Sandor asked. "How far did you go?"

Erika hesitated. She had to tell them about the rent, but she wanted to lead them to it gently. This didn't feel like the right moment to bring up Hart Latham's name. "All over," she said vaguely. "I don't know how Virag got out. We'd better check the fence tomorrow." *If we aren't busy packing*, she thought grimly. It

25

seemed like everything she said led straight back to Latham's ultimatum.

"I thought you fixed that fence last week," Papa said to Sandor. "We can't have that cow roaming loose!"

"I did fix it," Sandor said. "But half the logs are rotten. We need a whole new fence."

"What we need is a farm of our own," Papa said. "When we find gold, we'll be able to buy one."

"So where did you go looking?" Sandor pressed. He was probably calculating the time that she'd wasted, traipsing over the countryside, Erika thought. He knew that she went exploring whenever she had the chance. To him, it didn't seem fair that she could wander off at will, while he spent his days crouched in the icy creek. She studied the plants and trees, gathered herbs, and formed a detailed mental map of the country where they had come to live. "First I went west to a big meadow full of daisies and buttercups. She wasn't there, so I went north along Glutton's Gulch. Then I cut across a couple of ravines, and—and I saw the most beautiful little filly!"

"Where did you see her?" Sandor asked.

This still didn't feel like a good time, but when would be? "In Hart Latham's corral," she said.

"Looking for Virag, I ended up by the ranch house."

Papa set down his fork. "I've told you to stay off of Latham's land! That man is trouble! As bad as the worst Austrian landlord."

"I know," Erika said. "I didn't mean to. I just wanted to find Virag and get her away from there as fast as I could. But then I came across this filly of Latham's that was limping pretty badly."

"What was wrong with her?" Sandor wanted to know.

"It looks like shinsore. I was trying to think what Naganya would do, when one of the ranch hands caught me and made me go up to the house to see Latham."

"And so you went?" Papa exclaimed. He gazed up at the ceiling, as though he was looking for help from the heavens.

"I didn't have a choice. And I thought I could convince him to let me help the filly before her leg gets any worse."

"So what happened?" Sandor asked, leaning forward.

"Latham didn't want to listen to me," she said slowly. "He got pretty angry, actually." She drew a deep breath and plunged ahead. "He thought I'd come to pay the rent."

For a moment there was a stunned silence. Then Papa exploded. "I told him last month! I said I might not have the next payment on time. I told him I'll pay him as soon as I can! With interest! All I need is time!"

"Papa," Erika said, "he told me if he doesn't get the rent by tomorrow morning, we'll have to leave."

Papa leaped up from the table. His chair overturned and clattered onto the floor. "That liar!" he cried. "He can't kick us out. This is American territory! He can't treat us this way in a free country!"

"Maybe we can talk him into accepting part of what we owe," Erika suggested. "We've got a little bit of gold—how much can we give him?"

"How dare he threaten us!" Papa raged. "Sending messages by a girl who's only fourteen years old! Why doesn't he speak to me face-to-face like a gentleman?"

"What did he tell you last month?" Sandor asked. "When you said the rent might be late."

Papa thumped his fist on the table. "He said nothing! Just looked at me with those greedy little eyes, like one of the emperor's men! I didn't come all the way to California to be treated like a serf!"

As Papa fumed in silence, Erika gathered up the

supper dishes, and Sandor began to whittle a chunk of kindling. Papa muttered and paced up and down the cabin. No one was any closer to solving their problem. *Perhaps*, Erika thought, *if Papa went to him humbly, Latham would compromise on the rent payments.* But compromise didn't come easily to Papa, she knew this well. To him, this landlord was no different from the powerful landholders of the Austrian empire who had controlled Hungary for so long. Papa had left Szolnok, their native village, rather than give in. They couldn't pack up and leave a second time. There had to be another way.

After a while Papa took the lantern and went out to check on Virag. Erika pulled up a chair close to the fire, holding her hands out to its welcome heat. Sandor looked up from his carving. "So what if the old goat throws us out," he said cheerfully. "It's summertime. We won't freeze. I'll build us a lean-to in case it rains."

"Don't tease!" she snapped. "This isn't funny!"

"I'm just being practical," Sandor said with a mischievous glint.

"Then help me think," Erika told him. "How are we going to get Latham to let us stay here?"

"Hart Latham," Sandor mused. "You know what his

name means in English? *Sziv*! Heart!" Sandor pointed to his chest.

"He doesn't have one," Erika said. "He didn't even care when I told him about Arany."

"Who's Arany?"

"That filly I told you about. She's the prettiest golden color."

"You named her? That's asking for trouble!"

"Why? What do you mean?"

"You're getting attached to her, and she isn't yours. She belongs to old Heartless. You know he'll sell her as soon as he gets the chance."

"I know," Erika said. "And if he can't sell her, he'll probably shoot her. That man doesn't care at all."

✳ Chapter Three ✳

In the morning Papa was subdued, and Erika guessed that he had awakened to the grim facts of their situation. Instead of rushing out to the diggings at sunrise, he went to the pasture with Sandor to fix the fence. Erika was alone in the cabin when she heard a knock on the door.

Peering out, she saw Maddox, the ranch hand whom she had met yesterday afternoon. "The boss sent me," he said gruffly. "He wants to see you and your papa."

"All right," Erika said. "We'll go in a little while."

The man didn't move. "The boss doesn't like to wait," he said.

Sighing, Erika walked out to the pasture behind the

shed, where Sandor and Papa were propping up the fence with a new log. Erika saw at a glance that their efforts wouldn't stop an enterprising cow like Virag.

"Papa?" she called.

He looked up, frowning. "Latham?" he asked.

Erika nodded. Without another word, Papa gathered up his tools. He and Sandor followed her back to the cabin. Not a trace was left of Papa's fierce, fighting spirit.

They formed a dreary, silent little procession. Maddox strode ahead of them, and they trailed behind, their steps heavy and reluctant. Erika's mind raced as she trudged along. If they used the right strategy, they could still convince old Heartless to give them another chance. They had about two ounces of gold right now —it was only a fraction of what they owed, but maybe Latham would accept it and let them stay for a few more days. He was so greedy that he'd never turn down money. How would it benefit him to turn them out? If the Nagys were forced to move, the shepherd's hut would stand empty, and Latham wouldn't collect anything at all.

As they approached the ranch house, Erika glimpsed Arany and the other mustangs grazing in the corral.

She wished that she could examine Arany's leg again. But Maddox hurried them around to the kitchen door and left them standing outside while he went to find Latham.

Once again Erika stood in front of the door beside some scraggly bushes. She shivered with a blend of dread and morning chill. But at least this time she was not alone. Sandor and Papa stood beside her, their eyes on the door.

"Papa," Erika ventured, "talk to him. Offer him something. We can give him a little."

"He won't turn us out," Papa promised. He lifted his head and straightened his shoulders resolutely. Erika's heart lifted with pride. *You can't keep a Nagy down*, she thought. Not for long, anyway!

Hart Latham thrust himself through the door and gave them a sweeping glare. "Well, Nagy, do you have the rent for me?" he demanded.

"We bring two ounce gold," Papa said. "More Saturday."

Latham gave a brusque laugh. It reminded Erika of the crack of a rifle. "All right, I'll take what you have," he said. "And I have a proposition for you."

Papa looked questioningly at Erika and Sandor.

What did he mean? "I don't understand either," Sandor told him in Hungarian. "Maybe he'll explain."

"I won't charge you people any more rent to stay in my cabin," Latham went on. "How would you like that?"

"What's he saying?" Papa asked. Erika shook her head, baffled. She must have misunderstood him, she thought. Latham's words didn't make any sense.

"He says he won't ask us to pay any more," Sandor said. "We can stay for free."

"And I'll pay him everything I owe, when I make my strike!" Papa exclaimed. "He doesn't have to worry about that! Tell him, Sandor!"

Before Sandor could interpret, Latham went on. "Instead of paying rent, you send your girl here to work for me."

For an instant Erika felt as though her heart had stopped. Then it began to flutter like a terrified bird beneath her ribs. Work for Latham? She couldn't think of it! Unless—could it be possible—would he let her take care of the horses? She could help Arany after all!

As Sandor turned Latham's words into Hungarian, Erika studied Papa's face. His brows lowered in fury. "A slave!" he burst out. "You want to buy my daughter! You want her to work for you like a serf in the old country!"

Sandor didn't interpret Papa's words. Instead he asked, "What kind of work do you want my sister to do?"

"It's my wife who wants her," Latham said. "She's lonely up here. She'd like a girl around the house. Your sister can scrub floors, wash clothes, help in the kitchen. My wife will tell her what to do."

It wasn't to help with the horses at all, Erika thought. She remembered the pretty, soft-spoken woman she'd seen the day before, so delicate and shy beside Latham's harshness.

"She wouldn't be a slave," Sandor told Papa in Hungarian. "She'd keep Latham's wife company."

"Sandor!" Erika protested. "What are you thinking?" Sandor turned to her pleadingly. "This is our way out, don't you see? We'll be able to keep the cabin."

Sandor was right. If she came to work at the ranch house, she could save her family from losing their home. Working for Mrs. Latham wouldn't be like working for Latham himself.

"You can scrub, can't you?" Latham asked sharply. "You're not afraid of a little hard work?"

"I can scrub and sew and cook," Erika said. "Anything she wants." Latham almost smiled. "Do you wash clothes?" he asked. "I hate for Maggie to do heavy washing."

Erika nodded. She held up her hands, roughened by long hours at the scrub board.

"What do you say, Nagy?" Latham asked Papa. "Will you send her over?"

"We had a farm in Hungary," Papa said. "My wife had a servant girl of her own. I can't send my daughter—"

"Please let me, Papa!" Erika broke in. "It will just be for a little while!"

Papa looked fierce, but he kept his voice calm. "You're not a serf for him to order around," he said. "You deserve a decent wage."

"The rent is my pay," Erika argued. "It's good pay, if you look at it that way."

"Quit your bohunk talk!" Latham snapped. "Is she going to work here or isn't she?"

Papa said nothing.

"Anya would want me to do this," Erika said firmly. "She'd say I'm old enough to help the family. And she'd say . . ." She searched for the exact words that

Anya would have chosen, ". . . she'd say, 'Erika, whatever happens, it will be an adventure!'"

"You really want to work here?" Papa asked her.

"Yes," she said simply. "I do."

Papa sighed. "Erika will come," he told Latham in his halting English. "But I get money. Then she stay home."

"You start tomorrow," Latham said, turning to Erika. "Come here, to the back door, first thing in the morning. You'll work till sundown and go home at night. Sundays you're off."

When Latham closed the door, Sandor gave a long whistle. "You're braver than I am," he said. "I don't think I could stand to work in that place! It looks like a dungeon!"

"I'll be fine," Erika said, trying to reassure herself. "I'll find out what it's like to live in the big house— that should be interesting."

Papa frowned. "It can't do you any good to be near a person like that," he muttered. "I wish things were different."

Erika paused as they passed the corral. "That's Arany," she said, pointing. "Isn't she beautiful?"

"She sure is," Sandor said. He held out his hand and

clicked his tongue, but Arany hugged the fence on the far side.

"Come on, Arany," Erika called. "Come say hello."

As if she understood every word, Arany lifted her head, pricked her ears forward, and trotted over. "She's still limping, see?" Erika said. "It's worse than yesterday."

"If I know you," Sandor said, "you'll fix her right up."

"And maybe working here, I'll get the chance," Erika replied.

✴ Chapter Four ✴

The next morning Erika rose with the first streaks of daylight. She heated an iron on the fire and pressed her blue gingham skirt and calico bodice. She loved the smell of the steam rising from the hot cloth and the fresh, new feeling of the ironed clothes when she put them on. Her blonde hair hung down her back in two thick braids tied with ribbons at the ends.

She was the family provider now, she thought proudly. Her work would pay for their shelter. Buoyed by her sense of responsibility, she walked straight and tall across the fields. Cutting across the ravines and scrambling over the log bridge, she reached the ranch house as a full golden sun burst through the morning mist.

When she approached the house, however, she found that it was harder and harder to take each step. The house loomed in front of her, cold and uninviting. Erika passed the corral with a nervous glance and made her way to the kitchen door. It stood wide open. It wasn't as though it welcomed her, she thought. No—it looked more like someone didn't care enough to close it properly. Calling upon all of her resolve, she stepped inside. A sense of neglect pervaded the room. A collection of rusted pans hung on the walls. The fireplace was caked with grease, and the floor looked like it hadn't been swept in weeks.

"Is anybody here?" she called.

Footsteps shuffled toward the door, and an old man hobbled into sight, leaning on a sturdy redwood stick. "So you're the new hired girl," he said kindly through a gap where several teeth had once been. "We don't see many pretty young faces around here, that's for sure! I'm Jess. Pleased to meet you, young lady!"

"I'm Erika Nagy," she said, holding out her hand. "I'm supposed to see Mrs. Latham."

"She'll be plenty glad to see you, too," Jess said. "She's a sweet one. She'll treat you fine. The boss—he's a different story, but he's out most of the time. Tending to business. He's got a whole crew of miners working for him down on the Stanislaus."

"Should I wait here for Mrs. Latham?" Erika asked.

"She's up in her drawing room," said Jess, showing no inclination to move. He went on talking, as though he was starved for an audience. "The boss, he came out here to ranch. Then come the Gold Rush, and everything changed. He still sells a few horses and cattle now and then, but there ain't enough hands to run the place no more. Everybody that can walk is down at the diggings." He tapped his stick on the stone floor. "Latham, he's like the rest of them, but more so. Gold is all he thinks about. He's got a bunch of Mexicans and Indians working half a dozen claims at once. He's down at the river every day, making sure they don't pocket no loose nuggets."

"I thought a miner can only work one claim at a time," Erika said, puzzled.

"True, true," Jess said. "But the boss makes his own rules. Who's to stop him?"

Erika shifted uneasily from foot to foot. Jess was full of interesting information, but she couldn't stand here listening to him all morning. She had to begin her first day of work.

Jess seemed to read her restlessness. "All right, I'll take you to meet the missus," he said. "This way. Follow me."

His stick thumping on the flagstones, he led her across a patio, up a narrow flight of steps, and into a sunlit parlor. It was a startling contrast to the dreary kitchen. Plants tumbled down from hanging pots in lush profusion. A canary hopped from perch to perch in its cage above the door, and against the far wall stood a tall, elegant stringed instrument. Erika had never seen anything so delicate.

Mrs. Latham rose with a whisper of skirts. Her face wore the same shy smile that Erika had seen that first evening. She held out a pale, slender hand. "I'm so glad you're here," she said softly. "You have no idea how glad I am!"

Erika took Mrs. Latham's hand. It was very soft and smooth. She was suddenly aware of her own work-roughened fingers and calloused palms.

"I'll leave you two ladies to get acquainted," Jess said. "I'll be down in the kitchen if you need me."

"How old are you, Erika?" Mrs. Latham asked as Jess thumped down the stairs.

"I'm fourteen."

"Fourteen—that's such a nice age to be," Mrs. Latham murmured. "I'm twenty-two. I'm turning into an old lady!"

"You don't look old, Mrs. Latham," Erika said truthfully. "You're very pretty."

Mrs. Latham flushed with pleasure. "Don't call me Mrs. Latham," she said. "That makes me feel even older. Call me Maggie."

"Maggie?" Erika said, testing the name on her tongue.

There was a pause. Erika wasn't sure what to say next.

"It's hard living out here," Maggie said, looking in Erika's eyes. "Lonely. I grew up back east, in Ohio. Right in the middle of a town."

Erika longed to find out how this sad, delicate young woman had ended up married to Hart Latham. But Anya always said that it was rude to pry into someone else's past. For now, at least, she'd keep the big questions to herself. But surely small questions were all right. She pointed to the instrument and asked, "Do you play that?"

"The harp? Yes, I do—a little." Maggie brushed her

hand over the strings, and the room filled with shimmering notes.

Erika caught her breath in delight. "Would you play something?" she asked eagerly.

"Would you like me to?" Maggie said, her eyes brightening. "I'm not used to playing for people—except Hart sometimes."

"I've never heard a harp before," Erika said. "Please."

Maggie sat on a stool in front of the harp. She played a few notes, like a swimmer testing the water, and broke into a soft, floating melody that made Erika think of wind through rushes by a stream. From its hanging cage the canary burst into song.

"Oh, that was beautiful!" Erika breathed when the music ended. "Could you play another one?"

Maggie smiled dreamily. A fountain of notes leaped and tumbled from beneath her hands. Erika leaned forward, entranced. Never in her life had she heard music like this. "Thank you," she said fervently when Maggie's hands came to rest at last. "It's wonderful!"

"Do you play an instrument?" Maggie asked. "The spinnet? The fiddle maybe?"

Erika shook her head.

"Oh well," Maggie sighed. "We should be talking

about work, I suppose. What sort do you do?"

What sort of work don't I do? Erika thought. Since
Anya died, all of the sewing, cooking, washing, and
housecleaning had fallen to her. She milked the cow,
churned the butter, and tended the garden. She even
made soap and candles.

"I can do anything you need in the house," Erika
said. "Would you like me to sweep? Wash clothes?
Make soup?"

"You can help with all of those things around here,"
Maggie said with a nod of approval. "You've probably
noticed the place is going to wrack and ruin."

Erika hadn't heard the phrase "wrack and ruin"
before, but remembering the kitchen, she guessed what
it meant. "What do you want me to do this morning?"
she asked.

Maggie hesitated. "This first morning let's just visit."

This time Erika was certain she had misunderstood.
"Visit?" she repeated. "Like company?"

Maggie looked down, embarrassed. "It's so nice to
have someone to talk to," she said. "To hear a voice in
the house—a girl's voice—it's such a relief!"

It was Erika's turn to feel uncertain. "What do you
want to talk about?" she asked.

"Tell me about yourself," Maggie said. "Where do you come from?"

"I come from Szolnok, in Hungary," Erika said. "Our village is very small. No one here ever heard of it."

"Szolnok," Maggie said, playing with the foreign syllables. "How did you get from Szolnok all the way to California?"

For a moment Erika closed her eyes, remembering. "First we went by wagon to Buda. We had never seen such a big city before! My *anya*—that means mama— and I, we spent a whole afternoon just looking in the shops! Dresses and dolls and lovely cakes—you could buy anything there! Then we went down the river in a boat, and we sailed in a ship across the ocean."

"The ocean!" Maggie exclaimed. "I've never even seen it, and you've actually sailed all the way across it!"

"My father and my brother were seasick," Erika said. "But after the first day Anya and I were fine. We got our sea legs—that's what the sailors called it." She giggled a little—even now the words sounded odd. "We would stand at the front of the ship and watch the waves and talk about America."

"Is that where you learned English?" Maggie asked. "On board the ship? From the sailors?"

"The sailors and the passengers," Erika said. "Sandor and I—Sandor's my brother—we learned a lot of English on the ship. It was something to do."

Maggie was silent a moment, as if she was taking in everything that Erika had told her. "What did your family do back in Hungary?" she asked at last. "Were you farmers?"

"We had a big farm," Erika said, "with cows and pigs and horses." Those horses seemed so out of reach now; they belonged to a life that was faraway and long ago. "My *naganya*, my grandmother, was a horse healer," she added. "I went with her to farms all around our village."

"Would you like to see the horses we have here?" Maggie asked.

"Oh, yes!" Erika exclaimed. "Can we go look at them now?"

"Of course." Maggie rose from the stool. "Let's go."

The song of the canary faded behind them as they made their way down twisting steps and across a series of courtyards. Maggie led the way into a wide, high-ceilinged hall with a cold fireplace at one end. Above the mantel hung a pair of gleaming rifles. Maggie opened the heavy front door, and they stepped out into the sunlight.

"Hart just has these four horses right now," Maggie explained when they stood at the corral fence. She pointed to the palominos. "This one I call Star, because of the marking on his forehead. And the smaller one is Pigeon—I don't know why—the name just came to me. The pinto over there is named Brutus."

"What about this one—the filly?" Erika asked.

"I haven't given her a name yet," Maggie said. "Nothing quite suits her."

"I call her Arany," Erika told her.

"What's that?" asked Maggie.

"Ah-RYE-ni," enunciated Erika. "It means gold in Hungarian. For her golden color."

"And the gold rush," Maggie added. "It's a good name."

Arany was being shy today. She stayed bunched together with the other horses, but she watched Erika and Maggie constantly. Little by little, as if she thought that no one would notice, she left the others and eased toward the fence. Suddenly she put on a burst of speed and butted her head against Erika's shoulder.

"She acts as if you're old friends," Maggie said, laughing.

"I feel as if we are," Erika admitted. "Do you know she has a bad leg?"

Maggie shook her head. "I don't really spend much time out here. The horses are pretty to look at, but I don't know much about them."

"See how she's standing?" Erika asked. "She's trying not to put weight on her right foreleg. That's the bad one."

"Oh, you're right," Maggie said. "What do you think is wrong?"

"It's—I don't know how to say it in English. A soreness in the bone. But I think I can help her."

"What do you need to do?" Maggie asked with interest.

"I need to put a—" Erika searched in vain for the English word, "a wrapping on her leg."

"You mean a poultice?" Maggie asked. "My mother used to make camphor poultices for my chest when I had a cold."

"Poultice," Erika repeated, to fix the word in her memory. "Like your mother made, but this is for horses. There's a plant I need—I saw some this morning by the log bridge. I'll show you."

Erika led Maggie to Glutton's Gulch to gather

waybread leaves and mud to make a thick plaster. At the house Erika mashed the leaves to bring out the juices, while Maggie tore an old nightgown into long strips for the windings. In the kitchen, where Jess was banging around preparing the midday meal, they collected a handful of carrots and apples. At last, when it was all ready, they went back to the corral and discovered that Arany was skittish. When Erika held out a carrot, she shied away as though she sensed a trick. She pranced nervously and stuck close to the other horses.

Erika waited patiently. She stood just inside of the gate and pretended that she wasn't interested in Arany at all. From the corner of her eye she saw the filly edge closer, so gradually that it seemed like it was almost by accident. Her curiosity was winning out again, conquering her fear. Finally, when Arany was only a few feet away, Erika spoke to her, coaxing with her voice, and held out the carrot again. Gently, Arany took it from her open hand. She nuzzled Erika's palm, asking for more.

"That was amazing, Erika," breathed Maggie.

Presenting another carrot with one hand, Erika seized Arany's halter with the other. "It will be easier if we take her to the barn," she told Maggie. "In a stall she can't get away."

Maggie held open the gate, and Erika led Arany out of the corral. At the first tug on the rope the filly shivered with apprehension, but when Erika spoke to her, she grew calm. Erika led her into the barn and settled her into the first stall. Arany stood quietly as Erika wound the moist strips of cloth around her foreleg. Erika carefully wrapped the leg, making sure that the poultice was firm and smooth but not too tight, so that Arany would be able to move freely.

"There," she said, getting onto her feet and brushing bits of straw from her skirt. "I'll check on her tonight before I go home."

"How does it work?" Maggie asked.

"I don't know for sure," Erika said. "Somehow the leaves bring coolness. And their juices go in through the horse's skin."

"And this plant—it grows here and in Hungary?"

Erika nodded. "I was so happy the first time I saw it here, from the wagon on our way up from San Francisco. A man told me white people planted it on purpose. The Indians call it 'white man's foot' because they see it wherever white people have walked."

"We must have had it back in Ohio, too," Maggie said, "but I never noticed."

"I keep finding other plants I knew back in the old country," Erika said. "It makes me feel at home here."

"I bet you could go into business," Maggie said. "You could take care of horses all around the diggings."

"That would make me happy," said Erika.

Suddenly, Erika looked up to see Hart Latham watching them.

"You're back already!" Maggie cried. "I didn't expect you till tonight!"

"I saw Millerfield at the bank," he said. "I need to go down to the diggings this afternoon."

"Then you'll be here to eat," Maggie said. "Jess is cooking something."

Latham didn't respond. "The crews haven't found anything worthwhile in three weeks," he said. "I'm going to move them downstream."

"Erika and I had a lovely morning," Maggie said. "She's been telling me about her travels."

"Well, don't spoil her," Latham said sharply. "She's here to work, not to have a good time!"

"She has been working," Maggie said quickly. "Did you know she's an expert at curing horses?"

Latham eyed Arany's bandaged leg and shook his head. "I don't put much faith in doctoring," he said. "But if that filly gets rid of her limp, she'll bring a good price."

Erika's heart sank. As soon as Arany's leg improved, some gold-fevered miner was bound to buy her and take her away. More than likely he'd treat her like a common pack mule.

The clang of a bell floated across the yard. "Dinner's ready!" Maggie said. "Let's see what Jess has for us today." She turned to Erika and added, "He'll save a plate for you. You can eat when we're done."

Erika found a currycomb and brush in the tack room and groomed Arany until her golden coat shone. Then she led her back to the corral.

"You're beautiful," she said, giving the filly a parting pat. "You're much too good for the diggings!"

★ Chapter Five ★

Each morning Erika headed to the ranch house, returning to the shepherd's hut after sundown. Papa and Sandor had moved to a new claim on Jonah's Branch, but it seemed no more promising than the last one. Now and then Papa talked about rumors of gold farther north, in the wild country along the Feather river. But miners were still making big strikes right here, and he wasn't ready to give up or move on.

To Erika's delight, Sandor and Papa welcomed her stories about the ranch house and its inhabitants. She told them about Jess and the stews he concocted, throwing in "a little of this and that," with enough salt to fill an ocean. She told them that Maddox, the ranch hand, had vanished one day, having run off to the diggings without a word. Latham hardly seemed to notice. He was so busy searching for better claims on the Stanislaus river that she rarely saw him. She was working for Maggie, not Latham—and most of the time it didn't feel like work at all.

On some days she and Maggie worked side by side, scrubbing and polishing, doing their best to brighten up the cheerless rooms of the big stone house. They mopped the courtyards, watered the plants, and scraped layers of grease off the pans in the kitchen. They cleaned the ashes from the fireplace and put vases of flowers on the mantel beneath Latham's rifles. Sometimes they sewed in Maggie's sunny drawing room—the only room in the house where Erika felt truly at ease. Billy Boy, the canary, caroled above them merrily.

Checking on the horses was a regular part of Erika's days. She changed Arany's poultice every morning, and gradually the filly's limp disappeared. Soon, when Erika slid her hands from knee to hoof, she felt no traces of heat or swelling. "No more treatment for you," she said with satisfaction. "You're fine."

Brutus, on the other hand, was limping badly.

Somehow he had acquired a four-inch cut on his left hind leg. He was a nervous, bad-tempered gelding, and Erika knew that he wouldn't be a good patient like the gentle Arany. The first time she bent to examine his wound he tried to kick her, and his hoof grazed her shoulder as she sprang out of range. He reminded her of a mean old cart horse she and Naganya had taken care of back in Szolnok. The cart horse had settled down when Naganya fed him a bucket of oats with molasses while she tended to him. To Erika's relief, the strategy worked with Brutus here in California. Horses were the same all over the world.

When Erika had finished bandaging the leg, Brutus sulked in a corner of the corral. The other horses were in a playful mood, and Erika and Maggie leaned against the corral fence watching them. Arany gave Pigeon a mischievous nip on his flank, and he chased her in wild circles. Suddenly she reversed direction, and she became the pursuer. Pigeon bolted as if he was afraid of her, but he kept glancing over his shoulder to check that she was still playing the game. Meanwhile, Star rolled in the dust, kicking his legs in glee.

"I think they're bored," Erika commented. "Would it be all right if we took a couple of them out for a ride?"

"Oh, I don't know," Maggie said, looking uneasy. "I'm not much of a rider."

Erika looked at the ground, trying to hide her disappointment. After a moment she couldn't help asking, "Could we go just for a little while, up to the ridge maybe?"

"I haven't been on a horse in years," Maggie admitted. "I'm not sure I'd remember what to do."

"My *naganya* always said there are some things you never forget," Erika told her. "Swimming is one. Riding a horse is another one."

Arany and Pigeon had abandoned their game. Pigeon was cropping grass near the fence. Arany stood with her head raised high. Her nostrils flared as if she was drawing in scents from the farthest hills.

"The thing is," Maggie said slowly, "back in Ohio I used to ride sidesaddle. There are only men's saddles here."

"Oh!" Erika said, suddenly understanding. "I've seen women ride sidesaddle, but I never learned how. In Szolnok the women always rode astride."

"Like boys?" Maggie asked, amazed.

"I never thought of it that way," Erika said. "It was just riding."

Maggie gave her a shy, slightly mischievous smile. "Would it be hard for me to learn, do you think?"

"No," Erika assured her. "It's probably easier than sidesaddle."

"Well," Maggie said, "the only way to know is to find out."

In the tack room they found everything that they needed—bits, bridles, and a pair of beautiful tooled leather saddles. Erika saddled Arany and helped Maggie saddle Star, the gentlest of the palominos. The horses pranced excitedly when they were led out of the corral, and Erika wondered if even Star would be too frisky today for Maggie. To her relief, he stood calmly as Maggie climbed into the saddle. Erika mounted Arany and fastened a lead rope to Star's bridle. "Ready?" she asked.

"Grip with your knees," Erika advised. "Try to lean back a little and relax—there, that's better. Now give him a little nudge with your heels—just lightly—and loosen the reins like this." She demonstrated, setting Arany off at a slow walk.

Maggie gave a little cry of dismay when Star began to move, but within moments she was grinning.

"There!" Erika exclaimed. "You're doing great!"

"It's hard to get used to," Maggie said. "I hope nobody sees me with my skirt bunched up like this!"

"We need to make some divided skirts," Erika said. "They look like skirts, but they wear like pants."

"Pants! Me?" Maggie gave a peal of laughter.

"Hold on tight—we'll go a little faster." Erika nudged Arany into a brisker walk. The filly quivered with eagerness, and Erika longed to let her break into a gallop. This was not the time, she reminded herself, glancing over at Maggie again. Perhaps some other day she'd find out what Arany could really do, given the chance. For now it was wonderful simply to be perched on the filly's back, feeling the supple movements of muscle and bone and the steady cadence of hooves on solid ground.

They reined in the horses at the top of the ridge. Dismounting, they took in the view. They could see down into the valley, with a ribbon of river curling far below. Above them rose a ring of mountains, their flanks thick with trees, clouds enfolding their peaks. Before she knew that the words were coming, Erika breathed, "My mother would have loved this! I wish she was here!"

"How long has it been?" Maggie asked gently.

"When did she pass on?"

"Last September," Erika said. "On our way here."

Maggie waited. Her quietness invited Erika to say more. "She would have been all right if we'd stayed in Pennsylvania like we planned in the beginning. Papa heard there were a lot of Hungarians in a town called Pittsburgh, and we were planning to join them.

"But when we crossed the ocean and arrived in Philadelphia, everyone was talking about gold across the country in California. Papa wanted to go, and Anya, my mother, said, 'Yes, Laszlo, let's try it! We'll see our brand-new country, and our children will grow up free.'"

"They said we could go by wagon across the plains and deserts and mountains, or we could take a ship south to Panama, go just ninety miles across it, and catch another ship up the coast to California. We talked it over, all four of us, and since we were used to ships, we all thought the Panama way sounded best. So that's what we did."

She stopped, not sure that she could tell the rest without tears. "So you took a ship," Maggie said—her voice was warm and caring.

"The voyage to Panama was fine," Erika went on.

"But crossing the land there was terrible. It was so hot! There were mosquitoes; they were everywhere, like thick clouds. And huge spiders! And snakes that came dripping down from the tree branches! But Anya, she kept finding things to like about it all. She'd point and say, 'Look at those purple flowers! Aren't they beautiful?' and 'Did you see that butterfly? You'd never see one like that in Szolnok!' Our first afternoon in the jungle we saw a big bird with a long tail, all red and green and yellow. Diego—our guide—paddled our canoe through the little rivers they have there. He said the bird was called a quetzal. Anya said Panama was a magical country to have beautiful birds like that."

Again Erika halted. How could she tell the rest, how could she say the words out loud? Yet somehow she ached to share the story. It was alive within her, yearning to get out. "On our third night Anya got sick," she continued. "Her head hurt. It was a steaming hot night, but she kept shivering and asking for blankets. Diego made her some tea out of leaves and berries, and it helped her feel better. But the next morning she was too weak to get out of her hammock. She wouldn't drink any more tea or eat any food. None of us knew what to do. Papa and Sandor and I sat with her all day, holding her hands, talking to her, talking about California and the wonderful things she'd see when we got there. Finally she said, 'I won't be there to see it with my eyes, but my spirit will be with all of you, wherever you go.' And a little later she just . . . closed her eyes and . . ." Erika turned away. She wiped her eyes with her sleeve, but the tears wouldn't stop falling.

"I'm so sorry," murmured Maggie. "You must miss her so much!"

"Oh, I do!" Erika said, her voice catching on a sob. "I pretend she's here sometimes. I pretend I'm talking to her and showing her things, and I try to think what she'd want me to be doing . . ."

"I know she'd be very proud of you," Maggie said. "She'd be so happy with who you are."

They were silent for a while, each lost in her own thoughts. The horses cropped the grass contentedly. "I suppose we should go back," Maggie said at last. "There's work to do."

This time Erika unfastened the lead rope and let Maggie ride on her own. Erika led the way, still keeping Arany to a walk, and Star followed at a smooth, steady pace. What would Anya think of

Maggie? Erika wondered. What would she say about Latham, and the ranch house, and Arany? Even now, after all these months, it was hard to believe that Anya would never be part of her new life in California.

✳ Chapter Six ✳

After that Erika made two long, divided skirts, and she and Maggie went riding almost every day. Maggie steadily gained confidence, and soon she could handle the jouncing of a full trot. One morning when she felt sure that Maggie was ready, Erika let the horses break into a glorious gallop. Arany seemed to take flight, her hooves skimming over the ground, her mane and tail streaming. Erika shouted with exhilaration, and behind her came Maggie's answering shout. *What could be better than this?* Erika asked herself. *What could possibly be better?*

"I knew it!" Erika exclaimed when they drew the horses to a stop at last. "I knew Arany could run!"

"That was wonderful!" Maggie cried. "I've never felt so free in all my life!"

They had stopped in the grassy hollow that Erika had discovered the afternoon when she hunted for Virag. They dismounted and let the horses rest after their exertion. Wading through the deep grass, Erika found a wide, flat rock that could serve as a seat.

"Are there mountains like this in Hungary?" Maggie asked, gazing up at the peaks above them.

Erika laughed and shook her head. "Mountains? Hardly! We lived on the plains. Flat as a table."

"Ohio is flat too," Maggie said. "Elyria, Ohio—that's where I come from."

"Why did you leave there?" Erika asked. She hoped that she wasn't prying. "Why did you come to California?"

Maggie looked into the distance, as though she was gathering her thoughts. "It's all so faraway," she said softly. "Across the mountains and deserts and prairies— I never imagined the land could be so huge! Somewhere faraway is the house where I grew up and the Presbyterian church and the school where I taught —what a different life it was! And my mother and father and my sisters—I've only had three letters since

I've been here. I don't suppose I'll ever see any of my family again."

She paused, and Erika thought that she might stop right there. But after a moment Maggie continued, "I taught at a school, and that summer I was going to get married. I was engaged to Adam Brown, the doctor's son." Her voice broke as she went on, "But he caught typhoid, helping his father on his rounds, and nothing could save him."

"Oh, Maggie," Erika murmured, "that's terrible!"

Maggie didn't seem to hear her. She went on talking, spreading out her story in the sunlight. "I felt like I was sleepwalking," she said. "I was moving, talking to people, doing all the things that had to be done, but part of me wasn't really there. When Hart Latham came courting, it didn't matter to me one way or the other. My father warned me against him. He said Hart was a hard man, and he'd never make me happy.

"But my mother said Hart Latham would make a good husband. He didn't drink, and he had money. He was the oldest, and when his father died, he got the biggest share of the farm and whatever they had in the bank. Mama said the world is a rough place, and a girl has to think about practical things—food on the table and a roof over her head. Hart worked hard, and he'd be a good provider.

"I knew my mother and father wanted the best for me, and I knew they were both right in what they said. But neither of them ever mentioned the one thing that began to matter for me—that Hart loved me. I saw it in his eyes when he would listen to me playing the harp. I didn't feel for him the way I felt for Adam, but there was nothing left for me in Elyria. Hart started talking about going out west. He told me I should marry him, and we'd make a new life out there. He'd made up his mind, he said—he wanted me to be his wife, and he wasn't going to give up. Finally I said yes. Three weeks after the wedding we were sailing down the Ohio river on a steamboat, heading west."

"Do you ever wish you'd stayed back there?" Erika asked carefully.

"I made my choice, and I try to do my best," Maggie said. "Hart loves me as much as he can love anyone." Later, as they rode back to the ranch house, Erika realized that Maggie had not answered her question.

They rode quietly, keeping the horses to a walk. Somehow Maggie's story had drained the exhilaration out of the morning. Back at the house Maggie went inside and left Erika to unsaddle the horses and rub them down. Erika sensed that Maggie wanted to be alone.

She was checking Brutus' injured leg when she heard hoofbeats and the creak of approaching wheels. A light wagon rattled into view, drawn by a skinny roan mare. Two men called a greeting as it drew up in front of the house. This was the first time that Erika had ever seen visitors at the Lathams' house, and she wondered what their errand might be. "Hello!" she called. "Mrs. Latham is inside—I'll get her."

"No need to trouble her," said the shorter man. He was dark skinned, with thick black hair. "Markham here wants to take a look at the horses."

Erika opened the gate, and the men stepped inside. "I'm Juan Espinoza," the dark man said with a friendly smile. "My friend Markham is planning an expedition up north. He needs to buy some horses right away."

Erika's heart lurched, but she fought to conceal her feelings. What if he wanted to buy Arany?

Markham was all business. He went straight to the horses and studied them one by one. "What's wrong with that big fellow?" he asked, pointing at Brutus.

"He's got a cut on his leg," Erika explained. "I've

been putting poultices on it."

"So she has!" said Juan Espinoza. "Looks like Latham's got himself a regular horse doctor!"

Markham shrugged and moved on to Star and Pigeon. He lifted their feet, ran his hands over their flanks, and inspected their teeth.

"What do you think of them?" Espinoza asked.

Markham shrugged again. "Let me take a good look at this little filly," he said. Erika could barely breathe as he inspected Arany from crown to tail. *Please, no!* she thought desperately. *Don't choose her!*

"I could use all four," Markham said. "But the pinto's lame, and the filly's a little on the small side. I'll have to think about it."

Maggie emerged from the house and hurried to join them. After another round of introductions Markham explained that he had some business in town.

"Will your husband be back this afternoon?" Espinoza asked.

"He's usually here before dark," Maggie said. "I know he'll want to talk to you."

"I'll come back later," Markham decided. "Too bad about the pinto, but maybe he'll sell me the palominos and throw in the filly as an extra."

Their voices faded as Maggie walked them back to the wagon. "Thank you, Mr. Markham. You, too, Mr. Espinoza. Yes, it's nice to meet you both . . ."

If only Arany's leg was still bandaged, Erika thought miserably. Markham would have passed her by if he thought that she was lame.

Erika remembered Sandor's warning, "You're getting attached to her, and she isn't yours." Arany was Latham's horse, and he was free to sell her as he chose. It was one of those things that she had to accept. *Accept it and put it out of your mind*, she scolded herself. *Don't think about it anymore.*

She went to Arany and leaned against her shoulder. The filly nuzzled her hand hopefully and then searched the empty pocket of her apron. "Later," Erika promised. "I'll bring you a treat."

The dinner bell clanged, and Erika gave Arany a parting pat. Swinging the gate closed behind her, she hurried to the kitchen.

"Hart will be so pleased if he can sell them all," Maggie said as they spooned up Jess' salty stew. "Of course, he won't sell unless he gets a good price."

"Won't you miss them?" Erika asked. "We won't be able to go out riding anymore."

"True," Maggie said. "But selling them is the whole idea. He'll get others in a while, and we can ride them."

Maggie didn't understand. She loved the freedom and excitement of riding, but she had no special feeling for any of the horses. She couldn't guess how Erika felt at the thought of losing Arany forever.

Maybe Arany's size will count against her, Erika told herself. *Maybe Markham only wants big, sturdy horses that can haul heavy bags of ore.* But if Markham knew horses as Erika thought that he did, he'd recognize Arany's gentleness and intelligence. She wasn't just an extra to be thrown in with the other horses.

Maggie had set aside that afternoon for sewing. But before she climbed the stairs to the drawing room Erika remembered her promise to take Arany a treat. "I'll be back in a minute," she told Maggie and rummaged in the kitchen for some carrots.

"I'll come too," Maggie said. "The sewing can wait." Together they crossed the yard to the corral, where four horses had been grazing less than an hour before.

Brutus and the palominos stood together, their heads up, pawing nervously. They acted as though something was wrong—and in a sickening instant Erika saw what it was. The gate stood open, and Arany was gone!

★ Chapter Seven ★

With a rush of panic, Erika flew to the gate and slammed it shut. "How did this happen?" Maggie wailed. "Didn't you close the gate?"

"Of course I closed it," Erika protested. She pointed to the latch. "Look! It's broken, see?"

Sure enough, the latch had finally given out. It dangled uselessly, and any enterprising horse could nudge the gate open from inside.

Maggie sank to the ground. She rocked back and forth, hugging her knees. "What will Hart say?" she moaned. "He'll be so angry! What am I going to do?"

Erika shuddered to think what Hart Latham would do if he came home and found Arany missing—

especially when Markham was coming back before dark to talk about buying her. Erika would be fired for sure, and she and Sandor and Papa would have nowhere to live. She felt like sitting on the ground with Maggie and wailing too.

But in her head she could almost hear Anya gently chiding her. "Crying won't do you any good," Anya would say. "Go out and do something!"

Erika fought to get her voice under control. "Arany can't be far," she said. "I'll go and find her."

A glimmer of hope appeared in Maggie's eyes. "Oh, please!" she exclaimed. "Can you bring her back before Hart gets home?"

"I'll try," she promised. "I'll ride Star. We'll catch up with her."

"I'll get Jess to fix the gate while you're gone," Maggie said. "Maybe Hart won't have to find out about any of this."

Erika saddled Star and coiled a length of rope around the saddle horn. She led the gelding out of the corral. Star pranced excitedly, happy to be out in the open again.

"How will you know where to look?" Maggie asked as Erika swung into the saddle.

"I'll find signs," Erika assured her. "I'll watch the ground."

Virag had given her plenty of practice, Erika thought as she set off in a slow, careful circle around the corral. The ground was dry, and at first she couldn't find any tracks. She traced a larger circle, but still she found nothing. The third circle brought her to the creek, Glutton's Gulch. There, in the damp earth at the water's edge, she spotted a clear set of hoofprints. Arany must have come down to drink and then continued on her way. A few yards farther ahead Erika saw tracks again, pointing north.

Until today most of Erika's exploring had been closer to the cabin, down near the southern end of Latham's land. Arany was leading her into country that she had never visited before. She rode across a series of fields dotted with Latham's grazing cattle. Farther on the land broke into steep, jagged hills, as though a giant had carved them at random with a set of oddly shaped chisels and files. Here and there Erika saw where Arany had stopped to crop the grass. Once she found a swirl of dried earth where the filly had flung herself down and rolled. Erika couldn't help smiling as she thought of Arany's delight at being on her own.

Leave it to Arany, she thought with a glow of pride. Star and Brutus and Pigeon had all stayed behind, even though they could have broken loose as well. Little Arany, with her endless curiosity, was the only one to venture out into the unknown.

Still, she would have to find her and bring her back. She'd promised Maggie.

At the top of a crest, a ridge of bald stone surging up from the earth, Arany's hoofprints disappeared. Erika guessed that she must have walked for some distance along the bare outcrop. Her heart sank. Again she guided Star in a circle while she searched the ground for clues. She found no tracks, but at last she spotted a long, black hair tangled in the sagebrush. It could have come from some other horse or even one of Latham's steers. But it might also be a hair from Arany's tail. "We're on her trail again!" she told Star, patting his neck.

The sun was beginning to sink when Star lifted his head, quickening his pace. He sniffed the air and let out a ringing neigh. A higher neigh answered far ahead. It was Arany's voice, Erika felt certain. "Let's go!" she cried, nudging Star forward with her heels. "Hurry up! There she is!"

Star broke into a fast, jolting trot. They bounced down one hill and climbed another, but when Arany neighed again, she still sounded faraway. Erika rode through a narrow canyon and reached the top of another crest. She reined Star to a quivering halt. He stood still, his sides heaving. "Arany!" Erika called. "Where are you?"

For a long moment she only heard the silence of the hills. A quail called in the underbrush, and from somewhere came the gurgle of running water. Then, once more, Arany neighed. She was a little closer this time but still far out of sight. It was as if the filly was playing a game, Erika thought—teasing, calling mischievously, leading her on. There was nothing to do but follow.

The gurgling grew louder. The earth was softer here, and Arany's hoofprints showed as deep and as clear as the lines on a map. The tracks led down a gully and vanished at the edge of a tumbling stream. Erika dismounted and searched back and forth along the bank, but she found nothing. Arany must have waded into the water. Did she head upstream or down?

"Arany!" she called again. "Stop playing now! Where are you?"

The stream bubbled and chattered. Then off to her left she heard the clatter of hooves on stones. Arany neighed, and Star neighed back.

Beside the stream grew a ponderosa pine, its trunk split and charred as though it had been struck by lightning. Erika looped Star's reins over a branch. She uncoiled the rope and set off on foot, picking her way among the rocks and bushes. As she rounded a bend in the stream, she saw Arany at last. Golden as sunlight, she stood in water up to her knees. She plunged her nose into the stream and flung up her head again, shaking off a shower of crystal drops. She looked boldly at Erika and whinnied a greeting as if to say, "Well! I thought you'd never get here!"

"Yes, you're having fun, aren't you?" Erika laughed. "That was quite a chase you led me on!"

Arany took a few splashing steps farther downstream, and Erika hurried along the bank to stay abreast of her. She kept her hands low, hoping that the filly wouldn't notice the rope. "I brought something nice, just for you!" she said, her voice soft and coaxing. "Come see! You'll love it!"

Arany stood still. She flicked her ears as though she was taking in Erika's words and weighing them carefully. "You're not coming out?" Erika asked. "I guess I'll have to get wet then."

As the filly watched, Erika kicked off her shoes and lifted her skirt to keep it dry. Gingerly, she stepped down from the grassy bank. In the first instant she gasped with shock at the icy touch of the water. Fighting the cold with every step, she waded deeper. The stones were slippery underfoot, and she felt carefully for solid ground as she edged her way forward. "Steady there, Arany," she murmured. "Hold still—just another minute . . ."

She was almost close enough to touch the filly now. She lifted her hand very slowly, holding out one of the carrots she had tucked into her apron. But instead of reaching for the treat, Arany shied playfully. Kicking up her heels, she scrambled away, stones crunching and rolling behind her.

"Ugh!" Erika cried in frustration. She made a fruitless lunge for Arany's halter, lost her balance, and fell sprawling into the creek.

Her leg scraped, the cold creeping up over her arms and shoulders, and Erika struggled to regain her bearings. She was glad Sandor hadn't seen her fall! She could picture him teasing her about trying out a new dance step. Well, she did have an audience. Arany was looking on, gazing in horsey amusement. "It's not funny!" Erika spluttered. "And it's all your fault!"

Churned up by Arany's hooves and by her own thrashings, the water had grown muddy and dark. But beside her among the rocks something sparkled. It might have been a trick of the light—but no, it was a pebble, shining bright yellow among the grays and browns around it. Erika reached through the dark, swirling water and picked it up.

The pebble was around the size of a pea, roughly round, and with a dent on one side. It was very smooth, polished to a shine by the rolling stream. But what really mattered was its color. Its yellow gleam riveted her gaze and captured her imagination. It was the yellow of crowns and coins and wedding rings. It was gold!

It couldn't be, she warned herself. It was probably fool's gold, like the lovely stones that had deceived Papa and Sandor. She wasn't silly enough to be taken in by a single yellow pebble. Even as she urged herself to stay calm, her hands scrabbled among the slick stones of the creek bottom, and her eyes searched for more yellow glimmers.

They seemed to be everywhere—some as tiny as rice grains, some mere specks of sand, and one almost as big as a shelled almond. Erika forgot the cold. She lost track of time. She even forgot that she needed to rope up Arany and take her back to the ranch. All she thought about was gold—glittering dreams scattered in the bed of this strange black water creek.

At last the cold overwhelmed her. Teeth chattering, her clothes streaming water and mud, Erika staggered up the bank and dropped onto the grass. She basked in the heavenly warmth of the sun and gazed with wonder at the glistening pebbles cupped between her hands. Fool's gold couldn't be so beautiful, so entrancing! This had to be the real thing—the golden glory that had lured them through the jungles of Panama and all the way to California.

She remembered how Sandor had tested the yellow pebbles back at the cabin. She picked up a stone and slid it back and forth between her front teeth. It felt as smooth as glass. That's what Sandor had been looking for, wasn't it? He wanted stones that were smooth, not gritty.

Was this really gold? It had to be! What would Papa and Sandor say when she showed them what she had found? They could pay their debt to Latham now. They could pay Joe Muldoon at the store. They could buy a farm of their own at last!

Erika stood up and wrung out as much water as she could from her sopping skirt. She folded a large leaf into a pocket shape and brushed the gold nuggets into it, tucking the leaf into her apron.

Glancing up, she found Arany watching her from a few yards away. Her coat shone with the luster of the gold in Erika's apron. "Did you know all along?" Erika asked. "It's as if you led me here on purpose!"

Arany pricked her ears in that way she had, as if she understood exactly what Erika was saying. For a wild moment Erika half expected her to answer. She stood quietly as Erika went to her and fastened the rope to her halter. Without protest, she followed Erika upstream to the pine tree where Star waited. Erika put Star's saddle onto Arany, cinching the girth as tightly as she could to fit the smaller horse. Riding Arany and leading Star, she set off for the ranch.

Erika loved Arany's smooth, easy gait and the way that she responded to every flick and touch of the reins. This might be their last ride together, a final ride to say good-bye. And what a farewell present Arany had given her! Here she was, perched on this beautiful sorrel filly, with an apron full of gold. Who could ever have imagined that the day would turn out like this!

Glowing with excitement, Erika headed the horses south toward Latham's place. Off to her right the sun was sinking rapidly. At the top of the stony crest, where she had almost lost Arany's trail, she reined the filly in to gaze at a magical purple sunset. If only Anya was here, she thought with a stab of longing. Anya would love these sunsets in California—they were like nothing they'd ever seen on the Hungarian plains. And Anya would be dazzled by the nuggets of gold and all that they promised for the future!

Without the sun to warm her, Erika's damp clothes hung cold and clammy around her body. The moon's gentle glow barely illuminated the ground in front of her. Somehow in her excitement over the gold she had forgotten the perils of nightfall. A coyote howled, and a finger of dread slithered down her spine. She shouldn't be out here alone. Cougars hunted at night, leaping on their prey from rocks or branches. She had to get herself and the horses back to the ranch as fast as she could.

"Hurry up!" she told Arany. She squeezed with her heels, and the filly surged forward with a new burst of speed.

They were down in a canyon now, a twisting hollow between high, rocky walls. There had been a canyon on the way to the black water creek, but now in the dimness the landscape looked eerily unfamiliar. *Perhaps when we get out of the canyon, I will recognize something*, she told herself. But when they finally emerged onto an open plateau, she felt even more uncertain than before. Without the sun to guide her, she wasn't even sure that she was still heading south.

She reined Arany to a stop and tried to think. The road ran to the west of the ranch, looping southward toward town. If she crossed it, she would know that she had gone off course and would be able to double back. But she hadn't seen the road or any other sign of human presence.

Arany's forefeet tapped the ground impatiently. She shook her head, giving the reins a tug. "You brought us up here," Erika said. "Do you know the way back?"

Arany tugged again, harder this time. Erika eased up on the reins and gave the filly her head. Arany set off with her smooth, purposeful gait, uphill and down, Star trailing after her. They splashed across a trickling stream that Erika didn't remember at all, and she wondered if Arany was playing another one of her mischievous games. But she had to admit to herself that she was thoroughly lost by now. She had no choice but to let Arany lead the way.

Maybe they only traveled half an hour. Perhaps it was an hour or more. Erika had completely lost track of time when she glimpsed a light up ahead. "Oh, Arany! What a wonderful horse you are!" she cried. Arany broke into a gliding canter, Star following close at her heels. The light bobbed unsteadily forward. Someone was running to meet them, carrying a lantern! But then, with a shiver of dismay, Erika realized that it was Hart Latham.

✱ Chapter Eight ✱

"Where have you been?" Latham asked. His voice was low, but it shook with anger.

I'm not afraid of you now, Erika thought fiercely. She had gold hidden in her apron pocket. The Nagys were going to be rich. They would stake a claim on the creek—on Blackwater Creek—and gather up all the gold that lay waiting beneath its tumbling waters. Then no one would ever bully them again.

"I went to find Arany," she said simply. "I brought her back."

"She should never have gotten out in the first place," Latham said, glaring from his circle of lantern light. "I hear you were the last one in the corral this morning. Don't you know how to latch a gate?"

Erika opened her mouth to defend herself. She wanted to tell him about the broken latch. But it could be dangerous to prolong the discussion. Suppose Latham started asking why her clothes were damp and where Arany had been when she found her? Suppose he suspected that Erika had found something important this afternoon, something valuable? The Nagys' claim would never be safe if Latham learned where it was.

Let him blame me for Arany's escape, Erika told herself. Why did it matter? She had to get away from the ranch and home to Sandor and Papa with her news!

"I'll be more careful," she promised.

"It's a little late for careful!" Latham growled. "That buyer, Markham, left an hour ago. I had nothing to show him but two geldings, one of them lame." His voice rose in outrage. "You were off with my two best horses!"

"I'm sorry," Erika said. But she wasn't sorry, not at all! Her heart leaped with joy, and she had to put her hand in front of her mouth so that Latham wouldn't see her smile. Markham had come and gone. Arany was safe!

Erika's elation only lasted a moment. "Get down," Latham ordered. "And don't bother coming back tomorrow. Not tomorrow or any other day!"

Erika slid from Arany's back. Latham snatched the reins from her hand and began to lead the horses to the corral. "Tell your father I want my rent money," he said over his shoulder. "Pay up or get out!"

Well, we can pay up now, Erika thought as she headed homeward. They could pay their debt to Latham and move to a place of their own. They'd never have to deal with old Heartless again.

A breeze sprang up, and she shivered in her damp clothes. She had found gold, but she had lost her job at the ranch. No longer would she go for rides with Maggie or sit sewing with her in that sunny drawing room with Billy Boy singing in his cage. And she'd never see Arany again! What would become of the little golden filly who had so magically lived up to her name?

Erika realized that she was very late for supper. Sandor and Papa must be worrying about what had happened to her. She slipped her hand into her apron and grinned to herself. They wouldn't complain about her lateness when she showed them her rough little bundle of pebbles!

As she started up the path to the cabin, George Washington brayed a greeting from the shed. Virag wasn't bawling; Sandor must have already milked her. She hoped that he had started supper too—she was suddenly very hungry.

The door flew open, and Papa stepped outside. "Erika! Thank God!" he cried. "I thought a cougar had gotten you!"

Erika hugged him happily. "I'm fine!" she exclaimed. "Better than fine! I've got something to show you!"

"Your clothes are wet!" Papa said. "You must be frozen!"

"I'm perfectly all right," she insisted, but it was a relief to stand in the warmth of the fire.

"Looks like you fell in a creek somewhere," Sandor observed.

"You're right, as a matter of fact," she told him. "The luckiest creek you ever saw."

Sandor and Papa watched as she took the folded leaf from her apron and spread it open on the plank table. They stared in astonishment at her little hoard of flecks and nuggets, winking in the firelight.

For a long moment no one spoke. Then Papa reached out and picked up a cluster of nuggets. He let them trickle through his fingers like sand. "You found all this?" he said in awe. "Yourself?"

"Not by myself," she said. "Arany helped me."

"Then it's on Latham's land," Sandor said, sighing. "The rich get richer."

"No!" Erika insisted. "It's an hour's ride north, past his fields. It's land that doesn't belong to anyone—we can stake a claim there, can't we?"

Papa rested his hands on the edge of the table. Erika knew that he was trying to stay calm, but his voice shook with excitement. "Let's not get our hopes up again," he said. "It might be more fool's gold."

"I thought about that," said Erika, crestfallen. "But it can't be—it's too beautiful!"

"We'll test it," Papa said. He stepped outside and came back a few moments later with two good-sized rocks. He chose the largest nugget, the one that reminded Erika of an almond, and laid it on one of the stones. Then he pounded it repeatedly with the other.

After a dozen heavy blows Papa held up the nugget triumphantly. "It's gold all right!" he cried. "Look—it's a little flat, but it didn't break! Not even a chip!"

They passed the nugget back and forth between them, marveling. "You can't break gold!" Papa said. "It's got strength."

"Tell us from the beginning," Sandor said. "Where did you find this? What were you doing out there?"

Piece by piece, interrupted by a barrage of questions, Erika told the story. She explained how she had followed Arany's trail and how Arany had led her to the gurgling stream. "I call it Blackwater Creek," she said, pronouncing the words carefully in English. "When it gets stirred up, the water seems dark and thick."

"Thick with gold!" Papa cried. "How long did it take you to gather all of this?"

"Not long. I was too cold to keep looking."

"This is amazing!" Sandor said. "Papa and I break our backs at the diggings and don't find a thing for weeks, and my little sister chases after some silly horse and sees the elephant!"

"We'll go tomorrow," Papa decided. "You show us the way, Erika. We'll take a good look around and stake a claim."

"And we won't care how cold the water is," Sandor added.

"One thing I forgot to tell you," Erika said suddenly.

"Latham fired me from my job."

"Good!" Papa said. "I wouldn't send you back there anyway. You're no one's maid anymore! This is the beginning of a different life for us Nagys!"

They set out at sunrise, Sandor leading George, who was loaded up with tools and supplies of food and water. Erika estimated that the trip to Blackwater Creek would take two hours. Soon they were among the strange broken hills where Erika had followed Arany's trail. She recognized the high, bare ridge where the filly's hoofprints had disappeared and the crest from which she'd first heard Arany's neigh in the distance. At last she held up her hand for silence. "Listen," she said. "Hear it? That's Blackwater Creek!"

There it was, the laughter of water playing over stones. The sound grew louder, drawing them like a piper's music, until they saw the lightning-blasted pine tree and the creek that lay before them. "It doesn't look black," Sandor said. "It's nice and clear."

"It was all churned up yesterday," Erika said. "Come on, I'll show you where I found the gold."

They tied George to the tree, and Erika led the way downstream to the spot where she had found Arany splashing and cavorting. They all heaped their shoes on the bank and waded into the water. In her excitement Erika hardly noticed the cold.

Papa and Sandor moved expertly up and down, studying the streambed section by section. Sandor loosened stones with his jackknife to search for the nuggets that could be hiding underneath. Papa went to work with his pan and shovel. He filled the pan with shovelfuls of sand, gravel, and water and gently tipped it back and forth. Sand and pebbles sloshed over the rim while he peered at the remaining contents, searching, hoping. Because gold was relatively heavy, miners had discovered that it stayed in the bottom of the pan after the sand and other pebbles were sluiced away.

At first Papa and Sandor shouted out whenever they found a gleaming nugget. But soon they fell silent and worked with fierce intensity. It was as though nothing mattered except their search for gold, and they feared that even speech would take them away from the task at hand.

By comparison, Erika's work was almost random. She scanned the pebbly creek bottom for sparkles of yellow, gathering them into her apron and watching with satisfaction as her little stash grew and grew. It reminded her of a game that she and Sandor used to play along the river back in Szolnok, collecting pretty stones and using them to build a tiny city on the grass. *This isn't a game*, she reminded herself. These pretty pebbles would build their future.

It was late afternoon before Papa straightened up and looked at the sky. "Before we leave, we need to stake our claim," he announced. "Look for some good sticks."

There was plenty of deadwood on the ground among the trees, and they had soon gathered four sturdy stakes. Papa marked off the claim, 30 paces on each side, and drove a stake in at each corner. The claim spanned Blackwater Creek and extended into the woods on each side. To prove that he was working the claim, Papa left his pick and shovel in plain view on the creek bank. Erika had been in California long enough to know the basic rules of mining. Most gold seekers respected these simple tokens as proof of a person's right to mine the staked patch of ground.

Papa took a scale from George's pack and poured the day's flecks and nuggets into the balance. "Fourteen ounces!" he said gleefully. "And this is just the start of it!"

"I guess we won't have to sell shovels after all," Sandor said, drying his knife and snapping it shut.

"We can pay the rent, that's for sure," Erika said. "We still owe forty-eight dollars."

"Sixteen dollars an ounce, that's the going rate," Sandor said. "We can drop off the rent on the way home."

"And pay off the store as soon as we go into town," Papa added. "No more debts! Our fortune is made!"

"Thanks to my wonderful little sister," Sandor said, beaming at her.

Erika grinned back in sheer delight. "Don't forget Arany," she added. "I only found it thanks to her."

⋆ Chapter Nine ⋆

On the way home Papa delegated Erika to deliver the rent to Hart Latham. He pointed out that she knew the ranch house better than any of them, and it seemed the most natural that she should be the one to go to the door. At first she balked like George on a hot day. "I don't want to see Latham again!" she protested. "Not after yesterday!"

"He'll be in a much better mood this time," Sandor said. "A few ounces of gold will cheer him up."

"Well, maybe he won't be there," Erika said. "I can give it to Maggie instead." She waved good-bye to Sandor and Papa and headed toward the ranch house. She sprinted around to the kitchen door.

Jess was stirring something in a steaming pot on the stove. He smiled in surprise when he saw Erika in the doorway. "Wasn't expecting you no more," he said, wiping his hands on his pants. "You come to see the missus?"

"Is she in her drawing room?" Erika asked hopefully.

Jess gestured upward. "Hear her?" he asked. "She's up there practicing."

The shimmering notes of Maggie's harp drifted down across the patio. Erika raced up the steps and slipped through the door. Too late, she saw that Maggie was not alone. Hart Latham sat in the far corner, listening. The music seemed to have a magical effect on him. His face looked calm, almost peaceful, in the waning light.

The instant that they caught sight of Erika the spell was shattered. Maggie lifted her hands from the strings, and the last notes quivered and died in the air. Maggie looked from Erika to her husband, as though she had no idea what to do. Latham's look of peace disappeared, and his usual scowl settled into place. "I told you we don't need you here anymore," he declared.

"I didn't come to work," Erika said. "I brought the rent."

From her apron pocket Erika drew a bulging leather pouch. Latham snatched it from her hand and poured the contents onto the table beside him. The shining nuggets bounced and rattled like beads from a broken string. Latham stared as though he hardly believed what he saw. He tested a nugget between his teeth.

"I thought your papa's claim was all played out," he said.

Erika shrugged. She turned to go, but Latham held her back. "Has he staked a new claim somewhere?" he asked.

Erika didn't like the tone of his question. She shrugged again. Maybe she could pretend she didn't understand his English.

"I said—has your father staked a new claim?" Latham raised his voice, as if shouting would help him break through to her.

"They moved to a new claim on Jonah's Branch," Erika said. It was true enough—they had moved, a week ago.

Maggie changed the subject. "It's good to see you, Erika," she said. "Maybe you could come visit me sometime."

"It's good to see you, too," Erika told her. She wished she could promise that she'd come back. She missed Maggie, but she knew that she was no longer welcome under Latham's roof.

Latham cupped a handful of gold flakes and nuggets, rolling them hungrily between his palms. "Wherever this came from," he said, half to himself, "you can bet there's a lot more."

Erika didn't reply. She clicked her tongue at Billy Boy. The canary watched her with his beady eyes as he hopped back and forth on his perch.

"Good-bye, Erika," Maggie said, her voice soft with regret.

"Good-bye," Erika answered. She thought of Maggie's home, back in faraway Ohio. How lonely she must be with only Hart Latham for company!

"Stay away from those horses," Latham called as she turned to go. "Don't go near that gate, you hear?"

The strains of the harp resumed as Erika hurried back down the steps. The music sounded lonely and forlorn. The delicate notes of the harp reminded Erika of falling tears.

Even with Latham's warning ringing in her ears,

Erika headed straight for the corral. She leaned on the fence and watched the horses, not daring to open the gate and go inside. There were only three left now— Arany, Star, and Brutus. Pigeon was gone. Markham must have bought him. Someone had taken the poultice off Brutus' leg, and he was limping badly. If Latham wanted to sell his horses, why didn't he take better care of them? Erika remembered what he'd said on her first day working at the ranch house, "I don't put much faith in doctoring." He just didn't care was more like it. He was too busy thinking about gold and getting rich.

Arany trotted over to the fence and rested her head on Erika's shoulder for a moment. "We've staked a new claim because of you," Erika whispered. "Pretty soon we'll have money to buy land of our own. Maybe we can buy you, too." Arany whinnied and edged even closer. *If only we had enough gold to buy Arany right now*, Erika thought, *before Latham sells her to the next horse trader who comes along.* But she couldn't let herself dream of such a thing. There were so many things that the family needed—a house of their own, land, a herd of cows. For now a horse like Arany was a luxury.

"Good-bye, little lady," she said, running her fingers through Arany's mane. "I hope I'll see you again." As she walked away, she saw Arany watching her intently. She seemed to be stretching every last moment from their farewell.

The long trip to and from Blackwater Creek wasted many precious hours of daylight, so Sandor suggested that they should make a temporary camp at the claim instead of traveling back and forth. When they left the cabin the next morning, they packed blankets, a lantern, and enough food to last for three days. Sandor and Papa took turns leading the mule, while Erika walked beside them with a reluctant Virag on a rope.

They set to work as soon as they reached the claim and gathered pieces of gold until it was too dark to see. Then they slept under the stars, to begin work again at dawn. Erika's hands were crinkled and sore from hours spent in the icy water. Her back ached from bending over to study the creek bottom and stooping to pick up sparkling golden pebbles along the bank. When she felt tired, she reminded herself of all the things they would be able to do with their newfound treasure. Hour by hour

George's saddlebags grew plump with the riches of Blackwater Creek.

By the third morning they had gathered up all of the pieces that were easy to see. Erika decided to take a break. She was sitting in the grass, drying her hands in the warmth of the sun, when she saw a flicker of movement off to her left. Peering closer, she caught sight of a little striped lizard as it darted into the underbrush. Erika pushed aside the bushes, hoping to get another glimpse of it. It blended in perfectly with the fallen twigs and tumbled leaves, and no matter how carefully she looked, there was no sign of it anywhere. She was about to turn away when her eyes fell on a sliver of gold nestled at the foot of a tree. Automatically, she bent to pick it up, but it wouldn't budge. It was wedged tightly among the roots, and she had to pry it loose. "Sandor!" she called. "Bring me your knife!"

Sandor hurried over with his jackknife and set to work. The tree roots had grown around the stone and refused to let it go. Finally, Sandor chipped away a piece of the root, and the stone sprang free.

It was the biggest nugget Erika had ever seen, almost the size of her fist. Dazzled, disbelieving, she weighed it in her hand. "It must be almost a pound!" she exclaimed. "Is it really gold, all the way through?"

"I've heard about nuggets like this, but I've never seen one before," said Papa, after he had examined it thoroughly. "It's real all right. What a find! We'll go home tonight, and tomorrow we'd better go to town. We need to have all our gold assayed at the bank. The banker will test it and weigh it and give us dollars."

Papa had always been reluctant to take Erika into Dreamer's Mile, the town that had sprung up like a mushroom near the Stanislaus river diggings. He said that it wasn't right for a young girl to be around a lot of rowdy, vulgar-mouthed miners. But he didn't argue this time when she insisted on going along. She had discovered their bonanza, she had helped every day at the claim, and she had found the biggest nugget of all. Of course she should go to the bank with Sandor and Papa to learn the value of all the gold they had collected.

★ Chapter Ten ★

Early the next morning they set off for Dreamer's Mile. Everything about the town was new, and hardly anything looked permanent. A few houses had been thrown together using lumber from riverboats that were abandoned when their crews and passengers reached the diggings. Most of the miners lived in tents. Even the saloon and Joe Muldoon's store were big canvas tents shored up by an assortment of wooden staves and beams. The single street was a path of beaten dirt running along the riverbank.

It wasn't much compared to a real village like Szolnok. But to Erika, after weeks of isolation at the cabin and the ranch house, a trip to Dreamer's Mile was a vacation. Papa hurried them past the saloon, noisy with talk and the clinking of glasses. Two young men lounged in the street, haggling over the price of a bony brown mule. A weather-beaten old miner was busy hammering at a contraption that looked like a big, shallow cradle. "That's a new way of extracting gold," Sandor explained. "You work it like a pan, but it's better—bigger and faster."

Erika walked as slowly as she could, taking in each new face and every bit of activity. The men with the mule watched her as she passed, and Papa glared them into silence.

The only substantial building in town was the bank. It looked like a big wooden box with a door facing the street. Two heavyset men, with pistols in their holsters, stood guard outside. Erika pulled back at the sight of them, but they nodded to Papa, and he motioned for her and Sandor to follow him inside.

The bank consisted of a large, square room, the back half partitioned off by a heavy iron gate fastened with a padlock. Jake Millerfield, the banker, looked up from a paper-strewn table. He was a stooped, middle-aged man with a pasty complexion. He broke into a smile at the sight of Erika.

"Well, Nagy, who have you got here?" he asked.

"Is my daughter," Papa said proudly in his halting English. He rested a hand on Erika's shoulder.

"Haven't seen you in a while," the banker went on. "Any luck at the diggings?"

Papa grinned. "Is good luck!" he exclaimed, setting his sack on the table. "Very good luck for Nagys."

"Let's see what we've got here," Millerfield said, suddenly all businesslike. "We'll set up a test. Come around back."

He led them outside to a glowing cookstove on the riverbank. On top of the stove stood a big cast-iron pot.

"What's in there?" Erika whispered as the banker lifted the lid.

"It's lye," Papa explained. "You know—like you use for making soap. It'll eat into most metals—but not even lye affects gold."

Carefully, using a long-handled ladle and standing far back from the stove, Millerfield emptied the sack into the pot. He set the lid back in place and built up the fire. "Give it a few minutes," he said. "Got to boil it a while."

Erika remembered how the nuggets had withstood

Papa's pounding back in the cabin. That test with the rocks couldn't lie, could it? Suppose Millerfield's lye test showed that they had come proudly into town with a sack of fool's gold!

On the stove the pot bubbled like a witch's brew in a fairy tale. At last Millerfield lifted the lid with a pair of tongs. He reached into the pot with his ladle. Erika leaned forward, her heart racing. Nestled in the ladle lay half a dozen nuggets! Despite the boiling lye, they shone yellow and pure.

"I knew it!" Sandor breathed. "We've got the real thing this time!"

Again and again Millerfield dipped the ladle into the pot, until he had removed every last flake and grain. A few of the pebbles had turned gritty and black, and he tossed them aside. The rest lay in front of them, a sparkling golden treasure. "Use this bucket in the river here," he told them, "and rinse the gold very carefully. Don't touch it with your hands till it's rinsed well— that lye will burn you bad."

It was a slow, painstaking process, but they were too excited to mind. Sandor filled and refilled the bucket, Papa swished flakes and nuggets through the water, and Erika gathered them back into the sack. At last they went inside again and were once more nodded in by the glowering guards.

"All right," Millerfield greeted them. "Let's see how much it's worth." He set up his scales and weighed the gold piece by piece, muttering to himself and writing numbers in a ledger. He saved Erika's giant nugget till the end. "One pound three ounces," he said as the pan of the scale plunged toward the tabletop. "That one's a beauty!"

Erika, Sandor, and Papa watched intently as the banker studied his ledger. He added up a column of figures and checked carefully before he gave the answer they all awaited. "You've got a total of three pounds ten ounces," he announced. "At the going rate of sixteen dollars an ounce, I'll give you nine hundred and twenty-eight dollars."

Papa nodded, but Erika repeated the banker's words in Hungarian to be certain that he understood. Nine hundred and twenty-eight dollars! She couldn't imagine so much money all in one place. Her mind spun when she tried to tally up all the things that they could buy. And there was still more gold at Blackwater Creek. If they dug down into the creek bottom, who knew what they might find? They had only begun to work the claim.

"Tell him to give us one hundred dollars today," Papa explained in Hungarian. "He can hold the rest for us here. I don't want to take any chances with being robbed."

This time Sandor did the interpreting. Millerfield agreed and counted out 100 dollars in gold and silver coins. Papa passed a handful of coins to Erika. "You and Sandor go over to the store while I finish up here," he said. "Pay what we owe and buy whatever you think we need."

"You two watch out," Millerfield warned as they turned to go. "This town is full of ruffians today."

"It's full of ruffians *every* day, isn't it?" Erika remarked to Sandor when they stood outside. "Look at all these people! They weren't here two hours ago."

The street was full of men now. A noisy crowd clustered outside of the saloon, and knots of two or three people stood all along the street. "I wonder what's going on," Sandor said. "Why aren't they busy at the diggings?"

Ignoring the commotion, they headed to the store up the street. Three men were inside sitting on crates and talking to the storekeeper, Joe Muldoon. With a jolt of recognition, Erika saw that one was Juan Espinoza, the dark-skinned man who had come with Markham to Latham's ranch. "Somebody's got to write to his widow," Espinoza was saying. "There's an address back in New York."

The other men shuffled uncomfortably and shook their heads. "I never did trust that Fournier," said one. He wore a bright-colored sash around his waist.

"Dirty French claim jumper," agreed the third man. A scar twisted at the corner of his mouth when he frowned.

Joe Muldoon looked up and waved a greeting. "You folks in town for the hanging?" he inquired cheerfully.

"What hanging?" Sandor asked curiously.

"You haven't heard?" Muldoon sounded amazed. "A Frenchman named Jacques Fournier shot Ned Green last night. They got in a fight over a claim at Beaver Tail Ford. The Frenchman said it was his—everybody knows he's a lying sneak. Anyway, he pulled out a pistol and shot Green in the chest. Now he's gonna swing for it."

"I wonder how many men have died over gold in the past year," Espinoza said. "Does anybody keep count?"

"Listen to our philosopher!" crowed the man with the sash. "Mining's too rough for you, Espinoza? I'll take your claim if you don't want it."

Espinoza didn't answer. The others continued talking about the murder and how two miners had tested the noose to be certain that it would hold. Erika edged closer to Sandor. "Let's pick out what we need and get out of here," she said in a low voice.

"You get the supplies," Sandor said. "I want to see what's going on. I'll meet you outside." Before she could protest, he slipped through the tent flap and disappeared.

Fine, Erika thought, straightening her shoulders. *I don't need you to take care of me!* Easing past the men, she made her way to the counter. "I am Laszlo Nagy's daughter. How much do we owe?" she asked. "We want to pay."

Joe Muldoon smiled at her and consulted his account book. "Twenty-six dollars and forty-one cents," he announced. "Have you got it?"

Erika counted out the coins and laid them on the counter. Behind her the men fell silent, suddenly watchful. "Looks like somebody made a strike!" Muldoon said, sweeping up the money. "Gonna stock up on some supplies while you're at it?"

"Yes," Erika said, "we'll need a few things."

"I've seen you before," Juan Espinoza said suddenly. "You bandaged up that pinto gelding of Latham's, didn't you?"

Erika nodded. Espinoza turned to the other men. "This young lady is a horse healer," he declared.

The others studied her doubtfully.

"I've got a big bay gelding that went lame last week," the man with the scar said at last. "I'll give you five dollars in gold if you can fix him up."

"I can take a look at him," Erika said. "I'll see what I can do."

"Hear that?" Joe Muldoon chortled. "Nothing shy about her, is there?"

"We need flour, molasses, pork, and beans," she said. "Other things too."

The storekeeper hurried to fill her order, measuring out her purchases and packing them up in a burlap sack. As she picked it up, Erika looked for the man with the scar, the one who had mentioned the lame gelding. But he and the others had gone, drawn like Sandor to the excitement outside.

There was no sign of Sandor when Erika stepped

back into the sunlight. The street was even more crowded now, and she had no idea where to look for him. Bit by bit, like a sluggish stream, the crowd made its way to the far end of the street, where it spread out over an open field. "Sandor!" Erika called, but there was no answer. She moved along the street with the crowd, calling as she went.

Beneath a solitary tree stood a platform. With a shudder, Erika realized that it was the gallows, where the Frenchman Fournier would hang.

Erika felt a hand on her arm. A red-faced man grinned down at her, puffing whiskey breath into her face. "That's a mighty good rope they've got," he said with a smirk. "They're gonna hang that Frenchy high!"

Erika wrenched free and stepped hurriedly away from him. "Sandor!" she called again. "Where are you?"

"What are you doing over here?" Sandor exclaimed in Hungarian from somewhere behind her. "I thought you were going to meet me by the store!"

"I thought so too!" she flung back. "You weren't there! I've been looking all over for you!"

"What sort of lingo is that they're speaking?" the whiskey-breathed man demanded. "That ain't even French!"

"It's bohunk," someone said with a sneer. "You ain't heard of bohunk before?"

"Erika! Sandor! There you are!" Papa pushed his way toward them, twisting and elbowing to reach them through the mass of people. He seized Erika's shoulders and turned her around to face him. "Don't look over there," he told her. "It's not right for you to see this!"

"It's going to start in a minute," Sandor said. "Can't we just—"

"No," Papa said. Driving them in front of him like a pair of straying cows, he herded them out of the field and back to the street. It was almost deserted now. All of Dreamer's Mile was gathered in the field to watch the hanging.

"But everybody else—" Sandor began.

"It isn't a festival!" Papa said fiercely. "It's a terrible thing to see them take a man's life! There was too much of that back in the old country."

"Yes, let's go," Erika pleaded. "I've seen enough already!"

"Come on," said Papa, unhitching the mule. "We're going home."

✴ Chapter Eleven ✴

"Tonight we'll have a feast!" Papa announced when they got back to the cabin. He spread Erika's purchases out on the table—pork, cheese, potatoes, even a fat, ripe melon. Erika gathered some peas and lettuce from her garden and picked a bunch of feathery parsley to make the meal look especially festive. Sandor milked Virag while she worked over the fire.

Papa sat at the table, making calculations. "For three hundred dollars we can buy a piece of land up in the hills," he said. "Another hundred or so will build us a house. We need a house and a good, solid barn—and ten, twenty cows to start out."

Sandor came in, stamping his feet and setting a pail of milk by the door. "We ought to have a hundred acres at least," he said. "Or a hundred and fifty, why not?"

"We'll add onto the house as we go along," Papa said. "We'll have a nice ranch house like Hart Latham's."

"No—bigger than his," said Sandor. "Let's put him in his place!"

Papa waved his hand expansively. "Another few days on that Blackwater Creek, I'll buy you five hundred acres and a castle!"

"So far we've only picked up the surface gold—the placer," Sandor pointed out. "We'll find more when we start digging."

"And when our section of the creek is played out, we'll stake another claim," Papa added. "We can explore—find out which is richer, upstream or down."

Erika listened as she set the table. She loved the excitement in their voices. All of Papa's dreams were coming true. A thriving farm, a big house—tonight anything seemed possible.

"We could buy a couple of horses for herding the cows," she suggested. "I'd take care of them and go riding every day."

"Why not?" Papa said. "We could use a horse or two."

"If I had a horse of my own . . ." Erika said, but she couldn't finish the thought.

"Of course you'll have your own horse!" Papa said, beaming. "What kind would you like?"

"What I'd really like . . ." She drew a deep breath. "I'd like us to buy Arany."

"The filly over at Latham's?" Sandor asked.

"The one that led me to Blackwater Creek," said Erika.

"She's yours!" Papa declared. "As soon as we buy a piece of land, I'll see Latham about your horse."

Erika's heart danced. She hardly tasted the food in front of her. Arany! Arany! The filly's name sang through her head. What glorious adventures they would have, exploring the countryside near and far. While on Arany's back she would discover streams and canyons, hilltops and valleys that she had never seen before. And she would never have to worry about getting lost. Arany knew how to find her way home.

"Tomorrow I'll go to the bank again," Papa said. "Mr. Millerfield handles land sales. Sandor, you come with me to speak English."

"What about finding more gold?" Sandor protested. "Let's go back and get everything we can."

"You have to sign a lot of papers to buy land in this country," Papa said. "We need to get started—it can take a long time."

"I have to take care of my garden," Erika said. "I haven't weeded in days! I can work here while you're in town."

"All right then," Sandor agreed reluctantly. "We'll take tomorrow off. But the next day we'll be back at Blackwater Creek."

After all the excitement of the past few days, Erika reveled in having a quiet morning to herself. She swept the cabin and went out to the garden to tackle the weeds. They had taken a fierce hold while she was off gathering golden pebbles, and now they had no intention of letting go. Erika tugged and chopped and dug the tangled roots out of the ground, but new weeds seemed to sprout even while she worked. At last the midday sun drove her indoors. She got out flour and yeast to mix a batch of bread dough. Before she could begin, she heard hoofbeats approaching the cabin.

For a moment she thought that it must be Sandor and Papa coming home early with George. But George's hooves were never that quick and light. Those were horses' hoofbeats. And it wasn't a lone horse approaching—there were two of them.

Erika went to the door and looked out. Up the path rode Maggie Latham on Star. And Erika was delighted to see that Arany frisked and pranced at the end of a rope tied to the horn of Star's saddle!

"Maggie!" Erika cried in delight. "I never expected to see you here!"

"Would you like to go for a ride?" Maggie asked. "It's such a lovely day."

Erika glanced at the sky. A fringe of black clouds hung over the mountains, but the sun was bright overhead. "It might rain later," she said, "but we should have time. Do you want to come in and have something to eat before we go?"

"No, thank you," Maggie said hastily. "I'm not hungry. Look, Arany missed you!"

Arany was straining at the rope, stretching her neck toward Erika where she stood. "Oh, Arany!" Erika said, laughing. "I missed you, too!" She had to call on all of her willpower not to announce to Maggie that Papa had promised to buy Arany for her. Nothing was certain yet, she reminded herself. The land and the house had to come first. No use talking about something that might not even happen.

Arany was already saddled and ready to go. Brushing away thoughts of weeding and baking, Erika sprang onto her back and slipped her feet into the stirrups. "Which way should we go?" she asked Maggie.

"Oh, I don't know," Maggie said. "Anywhere you want."

Erika could tell that Arany hadn't been ridden in days—probably not since the afternoon that she had escaped from the corral. The filly was bursting with energy. As soon as Maggie unfastened her from Star, she leaped forward and left the gelding in the dust. "Whoa there!" Erika cried, laughing. She slowed Arany down long enough for Star to catch up. Then the filly was off again, glancing mischievously over her shoulder to make sure that Star was still behind her.

Maggie seemed happy to let Arany take the lead. She was a confident rider now, sitting gracefully in the saddle with a firm hold on the reins. They cantered across Latham's fields, past a herd of grazing cattle. Slowing to a brisk walk, they made their way along a narrow cleft between two hills. Then they were in open country, picking up speed once more. The ride was so exhilarating that for a little while Erika didn't think about where they were heading and simply let Arany choose her own way. Suddenly she recognized the jaggedly chiseled rocks of the broken hills north of Latham's ranch.

"I've never been up this way," Maggie said. "Is this where you found Arany when she got loose?"

"Not exactly," Erika said. Somehow Maggie's question made her uneasy. She tried to change the subject. "Look at that bush—those leaves are good for cooking. I don't know what it's called in English."

"It could be sage," Maggie said, but she hardly glaced at it. She seemed anxious and rushed, even though they were on a pleasure outing.

They rode on for a few minutes before Maggie spoke again. "Where was she? Can you show me?"

Erika's hands tightened on the reins. "It's pretty far," she said. "Let's not go all that way."

"We have plenty of time," Maggie insisted. "It would be nice to see some new country."

Maggie didn't look as though she had plenty of time.

She seemed tense and hurried, as if somewhere a clock was ticking out the seconds. Something wasn't right.

"Why does it matter where we go?" Erika asked. "See that canyon down there? Let's go that way."

"I just thought you could show me where you went by yourself that time," Maggie said. "I don't know why you won't." She sounded petulant, like a disappointed child.

Erika drew Arany to a stop. She turned in the saddle to look Maggie in the face. "What is going on?" she asked. "Why do you want to go there so much?"

To Erika's dismay, Maggie's face seemed to crumple. Her lips trembled, and tears slid down her cheeks. "Hart wants me to go," she said in a quavering voice. "He thinks you found gold, and he wants to know where."

"So he sent you to find out?" Erika asked, astonished.

"Yes. He told me to pretend it was just an ordinary ride and get you to take me to the gold. He's convinced himself it's on land he owns."

Erika remembered Latham's questions the day that she brought him the rent. She'd assured him that Papa and Sandor were still working a claim at Jonah's

Branch. But perhaps he had pieced together the truth. "I found Arany when I went looking for her. What makes him so sure I found gold that day too?"

"He asked the men at the diggings," Maggie explained. "They told him your father and your brother had stopped going to Jonah's Branch. The last day they went there was the day Arany got out of the corral."

"He told you to spy on me," Erika said. "And you agreed to do it!"

"I'm sorry! I shouldn't have! It wasn't right." Maggie began to cry in earnest.

Erika felt a surge of anger. "I thought we were friends!" she said. "Friends don't spy on each other!"

"I'm so sorry, Erika," Maggie sobbed. "How can you ever trust me again?"

Erika felt her anger ebb away. Maggie looked so forlorn and helpless. How could she stand up to Hart Latham? She had simply done what her husband ordered her to do. "It's all right," Erika said soothingly. "Don't worry. I'm not angry, not really." *But you're right, Maggie,* she added to herself. *I can't trust you. I can't tell you about Blackwater Creek.*

From somewhere in the distance came an ominous

roll of thunder. The fringe of clouds was thicker now, and it hung low overhead. "We better go back," Erika said. "There's a storm coming."

The rain began as they reached the ranch house. Lashed by the wind, it came down as hard and as driving as a barrage of bullets. They put the horses into the barn and gave them a good rubdown. Erika hoped that the storm would subside so that she could get home, but the rain came down as hard as ever. "Maybe you should wait here till it stops," Maggie suggested.

The barn was dry and warm, but Erika had no wish to linger on Latham's territory. "I'll be all right," she insisted. "It's only water." Waving good-bye, she stepped alone out into the storm.

⋆ Chapter Twelve ⋆

Lowering her head into the storm, Erika began to run. The wind lashed her face, and her rain-soaked skirt clung heavily to her legs. *Soon I'll be home,* she told herself. Papa and Sandor would be there by now, and they'd have the fire going. She would be warm, dry, and safe.

But no smoke curled from the cabin chimney when Erika dashed up the path. Virag mooed a mournful greeting at the pasture gate. Casting Erika a look of outraged dignity, she walked ahead of her into the shed. Erika rubbed her dry, did the evening milking, and forked some hay into the feed bin. As she worked, she realized that Maggie would always be under her husband's control. Erika knew, without a doubt, that their friendship would never be the same.

Sandor and Papa should have been back from town. Erika wondered what was keeping them so long.

By the time she entered the cabin, her hands were so cold that she could hardly light the fire. At last a glimmer of warmth crept into the room. She felt much better after she climbed to the loft and slipped into dry clothes. She was hanging her wet things by the fire when she saw the note. It was tucked beneath a mug on the table, a single folded sheet written in Sandor's scrawling Hungarian. "Papa and I came home to look for you, but you weren't here. We're off to see some land up the valley. A man called Juan Espinoza wants to sell it. Back tonight. Sandor."

Outside the wind howled, hurling fistfuls of rain against the cabin walls. *How far up the valley have they gone?* Erika wondered. In this storm they might have a hard time getting back. They might not even be able to get home until morning.

For a long time Erika sat before the fire, gazing into the dancing flames. She strained to catch the sound of George's hoofbeats and the voices of Sandor and Papa on the path. She heard only the pounding of rain on the roof and the shrieking of the wind.

Very soon now they were going to have land of their own, she thought, with a glow of happiness. A family with land was a family with roots, a family that belonged. The Nagys would make a home in this extraordinary new country and win the respect of their American neighbors.

But even when they owned land, would people still think of them as foreigners? With a shiver, Erika remembered the crowd in Dreamer's Mile and the field where the gallows stood. She thought of the miners who had torn themselves away from their endless search for gold, just to see the Frenchman die. The men in the store had spoken as though being a foreigner went hand in hand with being a murdering claim jumper. She remembered the sneering voice in the field when she and Sandor were speaking Hungarian: "That's bohunk! You ain't heard of bohunk before?"

A mighty gust of wind shook the cabin on its foundation. Sandor and Papa couldn't possibly get home tonight, Erika decided. She rose and bolted the door. In all her life she had never spent a night completely alone. *Of course there is nothing to be afraid of,* she told herself. She spent plenty of time alone during the day—why should nighttime be any different?

She sang a jaunty melody as she encouraged the fire with more kindling. Her voice filled the empty room—a defiant answer to the storm. When she ran out of songs, she recited a poem that she had memorized in school long ago, about the great King Stephan and his heroic deeds. But when she was quiet, the rain swelled to fill the silence, and the wind clawed at the cracks like a hungry stranger trying to find a way inside.

Up in the loft Erika lay awake for a long time, the events of the day tumbling through her mind. When she finally fell asleep, her thoughts twisted themselves into nightmares. She was in Dreamer's Mile, and a silent funeral procession filed along the street. Six men carried the coffin. "Who's being buried?" she asked the pallbearers. One of them turned to her and said quietly, "You know." Suddenly she did know. It was her own father they were about to lay in the ground. Anya was gone, and now Papa was gone too. She and Sandor were orphans. They were on their own in a hostile country, thousands of miles from anyone who cared about them.

She awoke with a jolt and heard the strange stillness that comes after a storm. The rain had stopped, and a few sleepy birds were calling. *It was only a dream*, she assured herself. Papa was alive and safe. This morning he and Sandor would come home full of news about Espinoza's farm. Soon they would be landholders like Hart Latham himself.

Erika scrambled down the ladder and stepped into the rain-soaked morning. Water dripped from the leaves, and puddles filled every depression in the ground. But the sun shone serenely, as though nothing had happened. She milked Virag and put her out to graze, propping up three logs in the fence that had toppled in the wind. Back in the cabin she renewed the fire and boiled water for tea. She was about to fry up some sausage for breakfast when she heard hoofbeats on the path. It didn't sound like George Washington, and she felt a cold knot of dread. There was a heavy knock on the door.

Hart Latham stood outside. With one hand he held Star and Arany by their reins. The other held a long-barreled hunting rifle. "Where's your father?" he demanded.

Erika stared in horror at the gun. For a moment she couldn't speak.

"I came to see your father," Latham repeated even louder.

"He isn't here," Erika said. "I don't know where he is."

Latham peered at her suspiciously. He stepped up onto the doorsill, out of the mud. "There are rumors going around," he said ominously. "People say your father's gold comes from a piece of land that belongs to me."

"It doesn't!" Erika protested. "It's nowhere near—"

"So he IS working a new claim! You told me he was still mining at Jonah's Branch!"

Erika couldn't pull her gaze away from the rifle. "My father isn't a claim jumper," she said.

"I won't know that for sure till you tell me where his claim is."

"Why did you bring a gun?" Erika asked.

Latham shrugged. "Coyotes," he said. "They got one of my calves last night." He paused and added, "Nobody takes anything that's mine and gets away with it."

"I'll tell Papa you were here," Erika said. "But I don't know when he'll be back."

"I don't like waiting," Latham said. "I especially don't like waiting for bohunks." Again he paused, adding weight to his words. "In fact, I might just go into town while I wait and form a posse. You know, it wouldn't take long to find your father and bring him in."

Erika clenched her hands into fists. *Latham is just trying to frighten you*, she told herself. He'd sent Maggie to collect the information that he wanted, and now he had come after it himself. She mustn't let him scare her. Somehow she had to stand firm.

But they'd brought in Fournier, the Frenchman— brought him in and hung him on that very day. Those same miners would be glad to go after another foreigner if Latham gave them the word. Had her terrible dream last night been a warning, a message about danger ahead?

"There's no reason to go after my father," Erika said, fighting to keep her voice steady. "He hasn't done anything wrong."

Latham shrugged. "The men in town can decide that," he said. "If you want to keep him out of trouble, show me where his claim is. You can ride the filly and lead the way."

An idea flashed into Erika's mind. She could lead Latham out into the hills and show him some other creek, pretending that her family's claim was somewhere along its banks. He wouldn't know the difference, and he'd leave them alone ... But of course he WOULD know the difference, as soon as he started panning. Then he'd be angrier than ever, knowing that he'd been tricked.

"Well, I've given you a chance," Latham said coldly. "I see you're not going to cooperate." He turned as if he was about to go. "The men at the diggings are cooperative when I ask them a favor. When I tell them to form a posse, they won't waste any time. We'll round up your father and that brother of yours too, while we're at it."

"They'll be back!" Erika insisted desperately. "Give them a little while—I know they'll be here soon."

Latham acted as though he hadn't heard her. "I guess you don't want to go for a ride today," he remarked. "I've been thinking of getting rid of this filly. She's not worth the hay it takes to feed her."

Erika stared, aghast, as he lifted the rifle to his

shoulder. "I might as well do it right now," he said, "and get it done before I go into town." He stepped down from the doorsill and maneuvered until the barrel of the gun pointed at Arany's head. In another moment a shot would rip through the air, and Arany's body would shudder and sag to the ground . . .

"No!" Erika cried. "Don't! You can't! Please!"

Latham held Arany in his sights. "Everything will be fine if you cooperate," he told Erika. "Show me your father's claim."

"It's not on your land," Erika insisted. "It's up in the broken hills, at Blackwater Creek!"

"Blackwater Creek?" Latham repeated. "Where's that? Show me."

"Put down the gun, and I will," Erika said.

Latham lowered the gun until it pointed harmlessly at the mud. "No funny business," he warned. "One thing I know about bohunks—they don't obey the laws in this country. They're nothing but lying sneaks."

He could fling ugly words at her all he wanted, but for the moment Erika knew that she had the upper hand. As long as she promised to lead him to Blackwater Creek, Latham wouldn't think about shooting Arany or rounding up a posse or anything else on earth. "I need a few minutes first," she told him. "I have to get ready." Let him wait, she thought. He hated waiting for foreigners, but he would have to wait for her.

Erika pulled a drawer open beneath the table and took out a pen and ink. She turned over Sandor's note and began to write on the back. Her hands had started to shake. She tried to write slowly and deliberately, but the words wavered across the page. "I've gone to Blackwater Creek. Latham is with me." She paused for a moment and then added, "He has a gun."

"Hurry up in there!" Latham shouted. "Let's go!"

Erika put down the pen. Her legs were trembling too. She stood still, struggling to get her body under control. She wasn't alone, she reminded herself. A friend would be with her. Arany.

Erika stepped outside and closed the door behind her. As he mounted Star, Latham threw Arany's reins in Erika's direction. They landed in the mud, and she had to stoop to retrieve them. Carefully, taking her time, she wiped them clean. At last she mounted the filly and nudged her into a brisk trot. She wanted to keep as much distance as she could between herself and Latham, and whenever Star began to catch up, she urged Arany to go faster.

Perhaps . . . perhaps Latham would soon see that Blackwater Creek was far north of his farthest field. But would that make a difference to him? Latham could talk about foreigners who didn't obey the law—but he was a man who liked to invent his own rules. Did Hart Latham respect any law besides his own?

Erika glanced back and saw Latham a few yards behind her. The rifle lay across the front of his saddle. It gave her a sick, shivery feeling. She could have held out if it wasn't for the gun. There it was, cruel and menacing. She knew that Latham would use it to get his own way. The rifle meant power.

Arany seemed to enjoy splashing through the puddles, as she had delighted in splashing in Blackwater Creek. She picked up her pace as they rode through the broken hills. Erika hardly had to tell her which way to go. She moved with confidence and purpose, along the bald, stony crest, over the next hill, down through the canyon. The filly seemed eager to show that she remembered every step of the way.

"You're not playing games with me, are you?" Latham demanded. "How much farther is it?"

"Just a little way," Erika said. "You can hear the creek

from here."

They reined in for a moment to listen. Instead of the soft gurgle that Erika remembered, she heard a grumbling roar. For an instant she wondered if they were headed for the right place after all. But from the top of the next rise she saw the ponderosa pine and then Blackwater Creek. Swollen from the rain, it rushed and frothed over its former banks. It rolled wide and fierce, a bold, angry torrent.

"There!" Erika cried. "This is where our gold comes from. This is Blackwater Creek!"

"I don't see any stakes," Latham said. "If your father's mining up here, where are his tools?"

Nothing about the place looked familiar except the lightning-scarred pine tree. Erika rode up and down, searching in vain. There was no trace of the pick and shovel that Papa had left. They must have been washed away by the rising water. The stakes seemed to be gone as well. Grinning with satisfaction, Latham watched her fruitless search.

"There!" she cried at last, pointing. "On the other side! There are two of our stakes."

"You need to use four," Latham said with a smirk. "Where are the other two?"

"They were on this side. The creek must have washed them out—I've never seen it so high before."

Latham snorted. "Two stakes and no tools—that's not much of a claim! I might as well drive in some stakes myself."

Now who is playing a game? Erika thought. Even if Papa's stakes had survived the storm, Latham wouldn't have cared. He would have created some other excuse to say that the Nagys had no right to mine here. And who could they turn to for help? Who would listen to foreigners over the richest man in town?

Latham dismounted and began to search for stakes. He was so eager to grab the claim for himself that he forgot about his rifle and propped it absently against a tree trunk. Erika watched him pick up a stick and jab it into the waterlogged soil.

"There's plenty of land for you to mine," she argued. "You can stake your own claim—we were here first!"

The roar of the stream drowned out her words. It didn't matter what she said anyway. No one would listen. Erika reached forward and rested her hand on Arany's neck. The filly turned her head to look at her. *You don't care where people come from, do you, Arany?* Erika thought. Arany only knew who treated her kindly, who let her run and explore, who loved her . . .

"There," said Latham, planting his second stake. "That's two."

He walked back toward the tree where the rifle leaned. In another moment he would pick it up, and then what might he do next? She had to distract him somehow. If she could keep him busy, maybe she could seize the gun herself. She'd never held a rifle in her life, but if she had Latham's gun in her possession, its power would be hers.

"You need four," Erika reminded him. "Those are ours on the other side."

Latham glared at her. "I'll take care of that," he growled. "I'll plant stakes over there too. This claim is mine—I'll swear to any judge and jury!"

Again Latham seemed to forget about the gun. He tossed a twig into the lunging water and watched it whirl downstream. Crouching, he dipped his hand in to feel the current. He straightened up with a frown and studied the opposite bank. Finally he came up with an idea. He remounted Star and urged the gelding toward the stream. But Star held back, tossing his head nervously. At the water's edge he refused to take another step.

Latham let out a string of curses. He gave Star a vicious kick. The gelding neighed and reared menacingly. For a moment Erika was sure that Latham would be thrown. But he yanked on the reins and managed to get Star under control. When the horse stood still, Latham slid to the ground.

I bet Arany would cross the stream if he was gentle with her, Erika thought. But she kept that idea to herself. Slipping from the filly's back, she watched Latham step into the water, leaning on a stick for balance. He didn't glance back as she stealthily made her way toward the rifle. He seemed so determined to replace the Nagys' stakes that he had cast aside all traces of common sense. The stream foamed wildly around his legs. In only a few steps he stood waist deep, where the water would have only reached his knees on an ordinary day. Erika thought of the slick rocks on the bottom. Today they would be more treacherous than ever. Step by step, Latham sloshed forward, his gaze fastened on the muddy bank ahead. Erika stretched out her hand, and her fingertips grazed the cold metal of the rifle's barrel.

Suddenly, Arany wheeled around, her ears pricked forward. She whinnied eagerly. From somewhere over the hill an answering whinny floated toward them.

"Who is it?" Erika exclaimed. She could see nothing, but she could hear the thud of hoofbeats. For a moment she forgot about Latham as she tried to imagine who might be riding this way. Then from the stream behind her came a mighty splash. Erika turned in time to see Hart Latham floundering in the water, all flailing legs and arms, his outraged shouts muffled by the water's roar.

✴ Chapter Thirteen ✴

For a few astonishing moments Erika couldn't decide which way to look. Galloping toward her came three mounted figures—two on horseback and one on a mule. Struggling onto his feet in Blackwater Creek, thrashing and hollering, was Hart Latham. Erika turned from one scene to the other, amazed, not quite daring to believe what she saw.

"Erika! What's going on?" It was Sandor—Sandor riding Latham's pinto gelding, Brutus. Beside him came Mr. Millerfield from the bank on a handsome bay. Behind them, Papa jounced along on George Washington.

"Sandor!" Erika cried. "Papa! Mr. Millerfield! I'm so glad you're here!"

Again she turned to watch Hart Latham. Water streaming from his beard and clothes, he staggered toward them up the bank. He looked smaller, as though the creek had washed away some of his bluster. He didn't remind Erika of a bear any longer. He looked more like a bedraggled goat.

"I found your note," Sandor said. "We rushed after you when we read it. Especially since Latham had a gun! What happened?"

Papa burst out in a deluge of Hungarian. "He forced you up here alone, at the point of a rifle! He should hang for this! Hanging is too merciful! Are you all right? He didn't hurt you? Thank heavens!" In English he bellowed, "How dare he!"

"I'm fine, Papa," Erika tried to assure him. "It was a little scary riding up here, but don't worry about me now."

"What are you doing up here, anyway?" Sandor wanted to know. "What happened?"

"He made me show him where our claim is," Erika explained, pointing at Latham. "Not at gunpoint, exactly. He didn't threaten to hurt me. But I was afraid for you and Papa and Arany, too."

Papa was asking more questions, and Sandor was trying to tell her about their ride from the cabin. For a while everyone was so busy asking and telling that it was hard to find out what had really happened. Inspired by the commotion, the horses whinnied greetings back and forth, and George joined in with a long-drawn bray.

Little by little, Erika pieced the story together. Sandor and Papa had gone up the valley to see the land that Juan Espinoza wanted to sell. On the way they crossed a dry creek bed. Later, when the storm broke, a flash flood turned it into a raging river. "There was no way to cross it unless you had wings!" Sandor exclaimed. "Espinoza said the water would go down after the storm, and he was right. But, meanwhile, we were stuck there, waiting it out."

"And hoping you were all right," Papa added. "I hated to think of you alone all night!"

By morning, the flood had subsided, and they hurried back to the cabin. Papa was frightened to find that Erika wasn't there, but then Sandor spotted her note on the table. Frantic with worry, they were about to set off for Blackwater Creek when Jake Millerfield rode by on his way to the ranch house. Millerfield told them that he was looking for Latham. Sandor explained that Latham was at Blackwater Creek, so Millerfield joined their expedition. On the way they stopped at the ranch house to borrow a horse for Sandor. Maggie let him take Brutus, "And he's a tough character," Sandor added. "Down in the canyon, he tried to throw me!"

"I'm so happy to see all three of you!" Erika kept saying. "I can't quite believe you're here!"

As they talked, Latham stood a little apart from them, dripping and glowering.

"Good morning, Hart!" Millerfield called brightly. "Looks like you've had a bit of a dunking!"

"It isn't funny!" Latham muttered. "I could have drowned!" He stamped his feet and tried to squeeze some of the water out of his clothes.

Millerfield dismounted and walked over to Latham. "I don't know what scheme you had in mind, dragging that poor girl up here, but I don't like the look of it. It almost looks as though you were planning to steal the Nagys' claim."

"I never—no! Of course not!" Latham stammered. "I don't need to take anything from anybody. I have a fine claim of my own!"

"Listen, I need to have a word with you," Millerfield went on. "It's not the most convenient place, but—"

"This is no time for talk!" Latham interrupted. "I'm half frozen!"

"It will only take a minute," Millerfield said. "Come over here," he gestured toward a clump of trees, "and we can have a bit of privacy."

"I'm going back to the house for some dry clothes!" Latham exclaimed.

"You don't care to speak in private?" Millerfield asked. "Then, we can talk right here. You're three weeks past due on your loan. When can I expect the first payment?"

"You can expect it," Latham snarled, "when my claim starts to pay off."

"Which claim? Your diggings on the Stanislaus have been played out for months!"

"I have a new claim," Latham said. "Right here at Indian Bend."

Millerfield shook his head. "It can't be right here," he said. "The Nagys have been working here for a week."

"I don't see any sign of it," Latham said. "I just staked it this morning."

"After Laszlo Nagy's daughter showed you the spot?" Millerfield enquired.

Latham stumbled in sudden confusion. "She just— I was—she—"

"Maybe you can explain it to me," Millerfield said, turning to Erika.

This is my chance, Erika thought, her heart racing. Now she could tell her story, and Jake Millerfield would set things right.

"Mr. Latham came to the door this morning," she said. "He thought we were mining on land that belongs to him. He said he could round up a posse to go after Papa and Sandor if I wouldn't show him where we'd found gold. So I had no choice but to bring him up here and show him our claim."

"She says it's theirs," Latham fumed. "But she can't prove it. No stakes, no tools, nothing."

Millerfield watched Erika steadily. "Two of our stakes washed away in the storm," she went on. "Papa's pick and shovel are gone too. Two of our stakes are still here, though. See them? On the other side."

"I see a couple of stakes on this side too," Millerfield said, puzzled. "Where did they come from?"

Erika pointed at Latham. "He just put them

there. And he was going to change the stakes across the creek."

"Until fate intervened," Millerfield said wryly, eyeing Latham's sopping clothes. "Justice works in mysterious ways."

"Justice!" Latham sneered. "You think you're the law around here, Jake Millerfield? Just because you run that little shack you call a bank!"

"I have a number of records in my possession," Millerfield said coolly. "Maps, deeds, ledgers. And I'm very familiar with the land up here at Indian Bend. A large piece of it belongs to me."

"You mean," Erika said in dismay, "Blackwater Creek is actually yours?"

"Not this section," Millerfield assured her. "This part of Indian Bend—or Blackwater Creek, as you call it— is free and clear. My land is upstream. It ends there, where you see that big granite boulder."

She looked. The boulder stood at a bend in the creek, a hundred feet upstream.

Millerfield turned back to Latham. "Really," he said, shaking his head again, "I didn't think you'd stoop to this! Trying to steal a claim!"

"You believe them?" Latham demanded. "You take

those people's word above mine?"

"Of course I do," Millerfield said. "I believe they're telling the truth. And now, you and I need to talk about our personal matter."

Latham had begun to shiver. Erika thought of the day that she rode back from Blackwater Creek, soaking wet and chilled to the bone. She almost felt sorry for him, standing in the wind.

"I can't pay you yet," Latham said somberly. "I haven't got the money."

"You borrowed from the bank to buy mining equipment and to hire workers," said Millerfield. "You listed your ranch as collateral on the loan. That means if you don't start to pay back, you'll forfeit the ranch."

"I'll give you part of it," Latham said, his voice almost pleading. "I can sell some of my cattle and the last of the horses."

"That would be fine," said Millerfield. "And pay me the rest in the next few months. We will draw up a schedule."

As they started to arrange the details, Erika walked over to Papa and Sandor. "Tell me about Espinoza's land," she said eagerly.

Papa beamed. "It's beautiful! Three big fields and a natural spring. There's a small house, too. We'll have to build a barn."

"All for five hundred and fifty dollars," Sandor added. "We thought he'd ask for more."

Their excitement was contagious. "Are we going to buy it?" Erika asked.

"We *did* buy it," said Papa. "It's ours!"

"We're landowners!" Sandor proclaimed. "We own land in America!"

"Five hundred and fifty dollars," Erika mused. "That leaves us enough to build a barn and buy some stock."

"Since the land cost less than we expected, we have extra money left over," Papa said. "How much does Latham want for that filly you're riding—your Arany?"

Erika gasped. "Papa—do you mean it? Can we buy her?"

"Of course we can! Find out the price."

Latham and Millerfield were still talking when Erika rode up to them. Millerfield smiled as she approached. "I have a question to ask you, Mr. Latham," she said, feeling very formal and grown-up. "What is your asking price for this horse?"

She couldn't read Latham's expression. He looked

149

both indignant and relieved at once. "I'll take forty dollars for her," he said after a moment.

"Why not sell off the other two while you've got the chance?" Millerfield suggested. "Make her a good offer, and she might take them all off your hands."

"A hundred dollars for the three of them," Latham said.

"No, I don't think so," Erika sighed. "Papa only said I could buy Arany."

"I'll give them to you for eighty then," Latham said impatiently. "It's a bargain!"

Papa was reluctant at first, but with Erika and Sandor interpreting, he finally settled on a price of 75 dollars for Arany, Star, and Brutus. Erika slid off Arany's back. She ran to Papa and flung her arms around him. "Oh, thank you!" she cried. "I can hardly believe it! I'm so happy—thank you!"

She went to Star and hugged his neck. Even Brutus got an affectionate pat. Maybe his temper would improve, now that she could finish treating that cut on his leg.

Finally she went back to Arany. "You're mine now!" she whispered in the filly's velvety ear. "You're really, really mine!"

Erika was almost too excited to listen when Jake Millerfield announced, "Mr. Latham will start working a claim farther downstream as soon as this high water goes down. There will be other miners up here too. The word will be out before you know it."

"But we can still work our own claim, can't we?" Sandor asked.

"Of course," said Millerfield with a nod. "You should get a bit more from it. Another three or four hundred dollars, I expect."

"Not enough for carriages and servants," Erika said in Hungarian.

"Enough to work our farm and earn a decent living," said Papa. "That's what we came here to do, remember?"

"I hope Anya can see all this," Erika said softly. "She promised she'd be with us in spirit."

"Always," Papa said.

"Always," Erika echoed, with a lump in her throat.

Sandor shifted uncomfortably. He didn't like shows of emotion. "Erika," he said suddenly, "I almost forgot to tell you! Juan Espinoza wants you to help with one of his horses."

"He does?" Erika asked. "What's wrong?"

"It's a mare, ready to drop her first foal. He thinks she's going to have a hard time with it—she's very nervous, acts like something isn't right. He wondered if you could tend to her."

"May I?" she asked Papa.

"Of course," he said. "Your *naganya* would be proud of you!"

"Where does Espinoza live? How do I get there?"

Sandor gave her hasty directions. It would be a long ride, more than ten miles. She had better start now.

One by one she thanked them before she left. She thanked Sandor for finding her note and hurrying to her rescue. She thanked Papa all over again for letting her buy Arany and the other horses. She thanked Jake Millerfield for setting the record straight about the Nagys' claim. She even waved good-bye to Hart Latham and told him to give her love to Maggie.

Then, at last, she sprang into the saddle and picked up the reins. Arany seemed to sense her excitement. She broke into a supple canter, floating like a bird over the hills. Erika touched her heels to the filly's flanks, and she put on a fresh burst of speed. She ran as she had never run before. Braids flying, Erika lifted her face to the wind, laughing with joy.

★   ★   ★

*To whet your appetite for another thrilling
adventure in the* Saddles, Stars, & Stripes *series,
read on for the opening chapter of*
Chance of a Lifetime.

★ SADDLES, STARS, & STRIPES ★

CHANCE OF A LIFETIME

DEBORAH KENT

MISSISSIPPI, 1863
AND THE CIVIL WAR RAGES ALL AROUND . . .

Returning home from a visit with her relatives, fourteen-year-old Jacquetta May Logan finds her family's plantation commandeered by the Union army. Alone in enemy territory with only Chance, her beloved bay gelding, for company, Jacquetta forges an unexpected friendship with a brave slave girl named Peace. Together, they devise a daring plan to rescue her family's Morgan horses and lead them to safety across the Mississippi river. But danger lurks at every step of the way . . .

✶ Chapter One ✶

Slowly, reluctantly, Jacquetta May Logan walked
from the barn back to the house. The July heat felt
dense, like a thick cloud she had to push aside with
every step. It had been deliciously cool in the
woods, where the leaves and branches filtered out
the rays of the sun. She'd ridden along a wide, shady
trail on her bay gelding, Chance, breathing in the
fresh air and grateful for half an hour away from the
sewing room. If only she could have gone on riding
till sundown, she thought. Aunt Clem would never
allow it, of course. There was too much work to be

done.

Sighing, Jacquetta slipped into the house through the side door. She crossed the hall and headed for the drawing room, where the sewing table waited, heaped with blue homespun ready to be made into clothes for the family at Brookmoor.

Aunt Clem was there to greet her. "Jacquetta May!" she exclaimed. "Where have you been?"

"I went for a ride—just a quick one," she said. "I've finished the bodice."

Aunt Clem frowned. "I see you have," she said, holding up Jacquetta's work. "If you hadn't been in such a hurry, you'd have remembered the sleeves."

Jacquetta felt her face flush. "I'm sorry," she said. "I'll do them now."

From the far end of the table Cousin Mattie offered a smile of sympathy. Jacquetta smiled back as she dropped into her seat. Dainty, golden-haired Mattie never slipped away from her work,

Jacquetta thought, no matter how tedious the task or stifling the room. Mattie's thread never tangled or broke. Her hems were always beautifully straight, and her seams were almost invisible. Her needle darted in and out, in and out, leaving a chain of perfect little stitches in its trail. It hurt Jacquetta's head just to watch her.

Jacquetta found her needle where she had stuck it into a scrap of cloth. With a will of its own, the thread twisted into a knot as she tried to slip the end through the needle's eye. Aunt Clem watched over her shoulder. "You're fourteen, aren't you?" she asked. "By fourteen, sewing should come as natural as breathing."

Jacquetta thought of the rake-thin, scowling sewing teacher at Miss Woodworth's Seminary for Young Ladies, the boarding school she had attended in Virginia. "At Miss Woodworth's they said I'll never be a seamstress," she admitted.

"What did they teach you then?" Aunt Clem wanted to know.

"French," Jacquetta said with a little shudder. "Elocution—reciting poetry and making speeches. And deportment. Deportment every day." She'd spent endless hours walking with books balanced on her head in order to keep her posture straight, practicing sitting and rising in her swirling skirts, and learning how and when to curtsy.

Aunt Clem shook her head. "All well and good," she said, "if these were ordinary times."

Jacquetta took up the panels of the bodice and pinned on the missing sleeves. If she wanted to take Chance out for a longer ride today, she'd have to finish a presentable piece of work. She'd do whatever she had to do for a few hours of freedom!

Aunt Clem took up her own sewing again to

set the right example. "We all have to work together," she declared, seated at the head of the table. "We're not just sewing for ourselves, remember. We're sewing for the Cause of the South!"

Jacquetta recognized the patient, resigned bow of Mattie's shoulders. After 17 years on this earth Mattie knew her mother pretty well. They were in for a lecture, and it might go on for hours.

"You girls should be proud of your heritage," Aunt Clem began, starting slowly, like a fiddler tuning up at a dance. "You come from the best stock in Mississippi. The Logans came out from Virginia when your grandfather was a little boy. They trace back to the best Virginia families too. The Washingtons and the Madisons are some of your own kin, don't forget that."

Whenever Aunt Clem started to talk about fine stock, Jacquetta couldn't help thinking about horses. The beautiful Morgans her father raised at Green Haven had a heritage to be proud of. Her papa had bought the stallion Samoset on a trip to New England, along with a string of Morgan mares. That had been back in 1849, the year Jacquetta was born. Now the Green Haven line was famous all over the South. You could tell well-bred horses by the way they held their heads high, by the grace and power of their movements. You couldn't miss their quick intelligence and eagerness to learn. Were there signs like that in people? Jacquetta wondered. If you lined up folks from three Mississippi families, could a stranger spot the Logans on account of their fine stock?

"That's why we're fighting this dreadful war," Aunt Clem went on, her voice rising. "The Yankees have no respect for our Southern heritage. They don't understand our way of life. And they think they can beat us." She struck the bell that stood beside her on the table and continued, "They think they can starve us out by blockading our ports. We can't import supplies, we can't sell our cotton, so they think they've got us in a corner. Well, they haven't got us. We'll make uniforms for our boys in the army. We'll make homespun clothes for ourselves. Every stitch we sew is an act of patriotism."

A black servant girl from the kitchen opened the door. "Yes'm?" she asked.

"Bring us some lemonade and some of Ella's fresh tarts," Aunt Clem told her. As the girl disappeared, she resumed, "We've all got to do our part. Even if it means doing chores we don't enjoy, we've got to pitch in for the Cause." Jacquetta struggled with her needle as Aunt Clem's words rattled around her. If you measured loyalty by how well a person did chores, she reflected, then she was a traitor to the Confederacy.

*

Aunt Clem's lecture finally ended when the servant girl came back with the tray. Sewing forgotten, Aunt Clem, Jacquetta, and Mattie moved onto the veranda for their well-earned refreshments. The spreading magnolia trees created a semblance of shade. Jacquetta breathed in the scent of honeysuckle and gazed out across the rolling fields. Half a dozen of Uncle Silas' Jersey cows grazed quietly in the distance, down near the brook that edged the woods.

"Well, Jacquetta," Aunt Clem said, passing the plate of tarts, "you've been here a week now, haven't you? It's so sweet of your mama to loan you to us."

"Thank you, ma'am," Jacquetta said politely. "It's lovely to be here." "Loan" was an apt word to describe the situation, she mused. Mattie had been unbearably lonely here at Brookmoor, and Aunt Clem had asked Jacquetta to come for an extended visit. Jacquetta was good company for Mattie, even though Mattie was three years older.

The tarts were delicious, each baked in a crisp golden shell and still warm from the oven. Jacquetta loved the contrast between the sweet pastries and the tangy lemonade. She leaned back in her wicker chair and listened to the joyful song of a mockingbird. It was so peaceful here at Brookmoor. She could almost forget about the men off fighting and the Yankees with their cannons and cavalry. She could pretend they were still living back in the days before the war, when everyone was safe.

But she couldn't pretend the war away. If it wasn't for the war, her brothers, Adam and Marcus, would still be home at Green Haven. She never stopped worrying about them. Had any news come? Was Mama crying again, while she, Jacquetta, munched tarts on Aunt Clem's veranda?

★

It wasn't right for her to be away at Brookmoor, where she didn't know if some new trouble had taken hold of her family at this very minute. Somehow the more she enjoyed her visit, the more she felt the need to go home again.

Away from the sewing table, Aunt Clem's natural warmth emerged. "Whatever happens, we've got to look for the silver lining," Aunt Clem remarked. "You're a silver lining for us in this war, Jacquetta May."

"Thank you," she said. "It's sweet of you to say so." After a moment she added, "Another silver lining is coming home from Virginia. The war let me get away from Miss Woodworth's."

It had felt like a miracle in February when Papa sent for her to come home, right in the middle of the semester. It was the answer to her prayers. There was too much fighting in Virginia, Papa wrote. It wasn't safe for her to be so far away. Not

that it was any safer in Mississippi, now that the
Yankees had Vicksburg under siege. Sometimes
they could hear the distant roar of cannon fire as
they sat on the veranda at Green Haven. That was
the real reason Papa had lent her to Aunt Clem
now. He thought Green Haven was becoming too
dangerous for his only daughter. Brookmoor was
ten miles south and farther inland from the
Mississippi river. The noise of cannons didn't reach
them here.

Jacquetta had been overjoyed to leave Miss
Woodworth's, to turn her back on French verbs
and elocution—and most of all on deportment
class. Sometimes Miss Woodworth's voice still
chimed inside her head: "Say 'Yes, ma'am' and 'No,
ma'am.'" "Curtsy when you leave the room." "Sit
up straight, Jacquetta! A lady always sits with her
ankles together." Now, on Aunt Clem's veranda,
she slid down in her chair and defiantly sprawled

her legs before her so that her ankles showed plainly beneath the edge of her skirts.

Hooves clattered on the drive, and the wagon rolled into view, with Uncle Silas perched on the seat. They hadn't expected him back from town until evening, bringing news and whatever supplies he could bargain for. He couldn't have gotten much business done in so short a time. Aunt Clem would start to scold and Uncle Silas would protest, and it all meant an end to these fragile moments of peace on the veranda.

Uncle Silas drew the wagon to a stop and climbed down slowly. Jacquetta saw that his hat was gone, and his hand trembled as he passed the reins to one of the stable boys. The boy began to unhitch the horses, a matching pair of black geldings named Jeff and Davis. Uncle Silas prized his team. He said President Jefferson Davis would be proud to know that such fine horses were named in his honor.

"Clementine!" Uncle Silas called. His voice cracked, and he tottered on his feet.

Aunt Clem sprang down from the veranda and rushed to meet him. "What's wrong, Silas?" she demanded. "What happened?"

"Grant's taken Vicksburg," he answered. "It's finished. They say in town—" He stopped, struggling for words. "They say blood ran in the streets. Like a river. A river of blood."

For a long, stunned moment no one spoke. Then Aunt Clem began to cry. She and Uncle Silas stood with their arms around each other, swaying together in grief. Mattie reached for Jacquetta's hand. Mattie was crying too, but Jacquetta felt too dazed even for tears. Marcus and Adam were in Vicksburg. Were they all right? Had Mama and Papa heard any news about them? And if Vicksburg was in the hands of the Yankees, what would happen to Green Haven, only seven miles away?

That night Ella, the cook, served up a generous dinner of fried chicken and sweet potatoes, but no one took more than a few bites. Jacquetta looked desperately from her aunt to her uncle, longing for them to assure her that everything would be all right. Their faces were haggard with pain and dread. They gave no comfort, only a sense of foreboding that she had never known before. She listened in horror as the dreadful possibilities unfolded before her.

"What's to stop them now?" Aunt Clem asked. "They'll burn our houses! Trample our crops and leave us all to starve!"

"Do you really think they'll come here, to Brookmoor?" Mattie asked.

"From Vicksburg they'll have the run of the country," Uncle Silas said grimly. "I'll burn my cotton before I let the Yankees get their hands on it!"

Mattie began to cry again. "We'll all be murdered! I hear they kill Rebel babies! They stick them on pitchforks!"

Aunt Clem looked furtively around the dining room and lowered her voice. "What worries me—they might stir up the Negroes. Get our own servants to turn against us."

"Servants" was the word genteel people used when they spoke about slaves, Jacquetta thought. They were fighting this terrible war over slavery, yet most of the people she knew didn't even like to use the word.

All of the windows were open, but it felt as if there wasn't enough air in the room. Jacquetta longed to escape. She filled her mind with a picture that made her happy. She was back at Green Haven, and none of this was happening.

The faces of her brothers floated before her. She heard Adam's teasing voice: "Go on, Jacquie! I dare you to jump over the pasture fence!" She brought Chance to a steady canter, and then they were up and over in a glide so smooth that she hardly felt the ground as they landed on the other side.

Chance had been a present for Jacquetta's 12th birthday. Back then he was a frolicking two-year-old colt who'd never felt a saddle on his back. Jacquetta used to bring treats for him out in the field—carrots and sugar lumps and slices of apples. She taught Chance to come when she whistled, like a big, friendly dog. Papa and Adam helped Jacquetta train him on the saddle. The first time Marcus saw her ride the frisky bay gelding he clapped his hands and said she was born for the saddle.

The bright pictures faded away. Where was Adam now? He'd volunteered last October, as soon as he turned 16. Marcus, two years older, had already been in uniform for a year. Her mind formed a hideous question, and she couldn't push it away. Had their blood flowed with that river in the streets of Vicksburg? She tried to imagine what they must have seen and heard—the roar of cannons, the choking clouds of smoke, the screams of men and horses dying in agony.

"I'm going back to the Mississippi Volunteers," Uncle Silas declared. "They've got to take me now."

"You can't!" Aunt Clem cried. "We need you here! Who's going to protect me and the girls?"

Uncle Silas seemed to expand in his chair at the head of the table. "The Mississippi Volunteers will defend our women and children," he promised. "Before the Yankees touch a blade of grass at Brookmoor, they'll have to contend with us."

At 61, Uncle Silas was almost 20 years older

than Aunt Clem, but that hadn't stopped him from trying to enlist when the war broke out two years ago, back in 1861. The recruiting officer had called him "Grandpap" and sent him home, angry and ashamed. It would be different this time, Jacquetta thought. They'd probably take any man who could hold a rifle. Her stomach gave a sickening lurch. They might even take Papa. His bad leg had kept him out of the war so far, but the army wouldn't be particular anymore. Papa wasn't like Uncle Silas; he hadn't wanted to send the boys to fight, and he hadn't wanted to go himself. He didn't talk much about patriotism and the Cause. Jacquetta almost believed he wished that the South had never left the Union, though he wouldn't say such a thing out loud. She couldn't imagine him in uniform, limping along with his regiment, firing a gun at fellow human beings, even if they were Yankees. And suppose he was wounded! Or even worse . . .

The words tumbled out before she knew what she was going to say. "Aunt Clem—Uncle Silas—I've got to go home!"

For the first time they turned their attention to her. "Don't you even think of it!" Aunt Clem exclaimed. "The roads aren't safe. Besides, there's no one to take you. You'll stay here with us till this is over."

"I need to see my family!" she insisted. "I should be with them."

"Green Haven is even closer to Vicksburg than we are," Uncle Silas pointed out. "It doesn't make sense to take you back; it'd be like putting you right into Yankee hands."

"We're family to you," Aunt Clem said, folding Jacquetta in her arms.

Uncle Silas added, "Keep our Mattie company. Your papa will send word. Just be patient."

Jacquetta fell silent, but her mind went on working. She had to get back to Green Haven somehow. She would leave tonight, even if she had to go in secret. Out in the barn Chance was waiting. She and Chance would find their way home together.